# BREAKING NEWS

## Also by Shirani Rajapakse

Chant of a Million Women (2017) (poetry)

I Exist. Therefore I Am. (2018) (short stories)

# Praise for *Breaking News*

## A 2010 Gratiaen Award shortlist

"Each story in the collection is located within a different social milieu, and yet, the author manages to do justice to each different social background she portrays. When she describes situations in which the main characters are the victims of violence, she manages to convey to the reader their emotions in powerfully descriptive language, which is poetic and nuanced. She does not merely use a linear narrative style but experiments with literary devices like flashbacks and at times employs overarching metaphors in some of her stories."

- Judges' Comments, Gratiaen Award 2010, Sri Lanka

"Humorous or heartbreaking, plain prose or philosophical, Rajapakse shows immense talent in this collection of stories. Readers will find it easy to finish the book in a single setting, but they will find it difficult to forget Rajapakse's elegant turn of phrase and the depth with which she tackles her plots and characters. While the majority of the media may focus on more prominent wars and military conflicts, the defeat of the Tamil Tigers marked the beginning of a new era in Sri Lanka and Rajapakse does her native country complete justice (and then some) with *Breaking News.*"

- Ekta R. Garg, Bookpleasures, USA

"The language is simple and unadorned, marked by a starkness exactly appropriate to the subject matter. The stories contain oblique descriptions of people and places, but pain and loss form the major chord in these related arias."

- Luke Sherwood, Basso Profundo, USA

SHIRANI RAJAPAKSE

# BREAKING NEWS

Cover image and design by FayeFayeDesigns
fiverr.com/fayefayedesigns

First Published in 2011

Second Print edition 2018
First ebook published in 2018

Paperback: ISBN: 978-955-38285-5-2
eBook: ISBN: 978-955-38285-2-1

1. Short Stories. 2. Fiction—21st century. 3. General. 4. Sri Lanka. 5. Literary Fiction. 6. Asian Writer. 7. Shirani Rajapakse.

For information about permission to reproduce selections from this book, or to translate, write to
shiraniraj@hotmail.com
shiranirajapakse@gmail.com
shiranirajapakse.wordpress.com

# CONTENTS

# Missing Pieces

There was something very wrong. He knew it the moment his foot touched the ground. His right foot. But he lifted it up anyway. The noise deafened him. It threw him away. Far away. And then he remembered no more.

He woke up to a searing pain in his leg. There was nothing where his leg had been, except the pain, incessant, searing, gripping. How could there be pain for something that didn't exist?

The sun mercilessly sprayed its rays down on him as he lay writhing in a cauldron of pain that seemed to turn and twist him in every direction. He tried to stand, but could not. Tried to sit, that too he could not. The others hovered around him, unsure how to react. They were new recruits just like him and although they had gone through the drill, the sudden shock of it all, to see one of their fellow travelers going through what they could only imagine made them balk. They stood over him, a human wall surrounding him, watching helplessly, not sure what to say or do. He heard someone say something that was lost in the howl of his pain.

Someone gestured, but that too was lost in the glare of the searing heat. The gesture flapped helplessly in the air and was seemingly lost in the breeze. They stood watching him, listening to him, their fear mounting. They were talking among themselves, asking him questions, telling him things, but it was all a whole lot of sounds that flew about the breeze. He heard, but didn't understand. They watched him on the ground. They had no idea what do to.

They must have stood there for an eternity. Then someone broke out of the trance and shouted out an order. The others awoke from their daze. They bent down to pick him up, whatever was left of him. He waited unmoving except in whatever direction the pain pushed him until someone pulled him up. Someone else picked him up. They dragged him away half crazed, dripping with blood like a carcass of a cow hung up on a hook inside the butchers shop.

Except that this was no dead cow but a man screaming to live.

The piece of leg that caught the full impact of the shock had long since disappeared: scattered all around the Vanni like specks of dust. Some had stuck to the leaves and branches of trees while the rest had just melted away, or so it seemed. There was nothing left to take except the remains of the man to which the leg belonged. They half dragged, half carried the now screaming, now fainting man almost half a mile to where the rest were waiting. They threw him into the jeep and tumbled in after him. He lay groaning, fainting and bleeding, covering the floor of the jeep brown red with his blood.

The engine roared to life and moved through the harsh terrain, retracing its path back to civilization. All the while, he lay there on the floor feeling every movement of the wheels as they moved over rocks and undergrowth and swayed past trees that seemed to appear in their path out of nowhere. Every time the wheels rolled a little closer to the destination, the pain moved a little harder inside him. He blacked out, regained consciousness, only to pass out again as the pain pushed deeper and deeper into him like an electric drill. He didn't know how many times he must have fainted. Every time he opened his eyes he saw the dark shroud of branches overhead and someone looking down at him with despair.

He made it to the hospital many miles away. He didn't know how long it took or how far he had travelled. But he got there somehow. They had managed to drive to the hospital without any incident. He was lucky, they said. Others didn't have it that easy. They sometimes had to wait for days in and out of pain, as progress out of the Vanni was frequently hampered by threats. They were treated by those around them, with whatever they had with them. But this wasn't always enough. If they were lucky they would make it through with the treatment, but if not, then they left their last breath in the Vanni.

He was one of the fortunate ones, or so they said, although he wondered how he was so. He woke up to see the bright white coats of the men who pulled him out and dumped him onto a stretcher. And then he blacked out again. He had arrived, but had no recollection of what transpired next. He woke up again to see the bright lights of the ward shining from afar, blinding him yet soothing him at the same time.

It was night and he was on a bed. Others like him lay in rows of beds all around, wounded, recuperating, in pain. The place was noisy as people talked to each other, to themselves, to no one in particular. The place was deadly silent as people shut themselves from the world, from the pain, from the here and now. They were together in this, yet also so alone. He too was one of them. He could neither speak nor shout. His silence screamed inside him, yet no words moved out of his mouth. He watched the lights shine brightly, too brightly as if trying to say it was really alright. The mattress was hard. He could feel it, yet sometimes he could not. He lay there staring, staring while his mind screamed.

They told him he was inside the ward. They told him they cut his leg off above the knee. He had lost the lower portion of his leg. The knee was badly damaged and the doctors thought it best to sever the part from his thigh. So there he was left with a stump where once a leg stuck out. Bandaged in rolls of white it thrust out from him like a large sore thumb. It hurt him to see it. He lifted his head from the pillow and stared down at the white stump sticking out next to his leg. He could feel his knee, his toes; feel the movement of his ankle the way it moved when he walked. He could even feel his toes as he wriggled them, counted them, one two three four five, yet when he looked down there was nothing. Not a single toe, no ankle no leg. He was feeling something, yet there was nothing. How could he feel nothing?

They had not prepared him for this. They had not said anything that could explain all this to him now. Nothing made sense just as nothing could be felt. Tears welled in his eyes, they poured down his cheeks in unaided streams to flow into the pillow and soak itself in the softness of the cotton therein. No one heard him cry. It was a noiseless sound, gurgling from the depth of his throat to move in silent waves out of his mouth. He cried to himself. He cried for the uselessness of it all. He cried in frustration, in bewilderment, in anguish, and he cried in anger at the man who had made it all happen. The megalomaniac that lived off the living every day; devoured their lives to sustain his dream of building castles in the jungle. Mostly he cried at the helplessness he was feeling, and things to come that he did not know of but could only fathom. There was no one there to care. They were all the same; starting off whole yet ending with missing pieces: sad rejects of a society that needed whole people, but had been shortchanged too soon.

He was in a room full of people with missing pieces. They were young, yet the one act that had brought them there had changed them overnight. They had grown so old in the space of a few days. Row upon row they lay like rag dolls with broken parts that could not be mended, with missing pieces that could not be found. They had lost them on the way, not of their will, but due to someone else's will; the megalomaniac dressed in stripes who wanted nothing but to kill, to destroy. So he got his boys to lay mines in the ground. Buried them underground and let them bide their time until an unsuspecting foot placed itself on the earth overhead. The mines would then wake up. The hard tread of the heavy booted foot on it was the signal. The moment the foot lifted, it too would lift off, taking with it whatever was in its way. No excuses. No releases. Just plain action. It rose out of the hardened earth to burst into flame like a Chinese fireworks display shooting off far, far above, defying gravity to reach, reach straight ahead, only to release itself in a voluminous display of color lighting up the dark night sky.

Only this wasn't a display of Chinese fireworks. There was nothing beautiful in it. Nothing awe inspiring. Just plain ugliness rising up to claim a limb, a life, a loved one, a dream. Soaring up and cracking into pieces, removing flesh, destroying flesh, searing and maiming. Every day it claimed someone and every day the megalomaniac got a little fatter on the blood he had spilt, the flesh he had ripped out.

He lay there for what seemed like an eternity. His family didn't come to see him. They lived far away, a world away from all that was happening around him. They didn't know what had happened to him until much later, and even then there was nothing they could do. What was the use? It was too far for them to travel. Too much money to spend on the travel. Where would they stay when they got there? They were poor. They wouldn't be able to do much for him now. There would be time yet when he returned home. So they made some excuse. Told him over the phone.

He understood, yet didn't quite comprehend.

The people dressed in white took care of him. They bathed and fed him for the first few days. Then when he was able to sit up in bed, they left him to learn to care for himself. They were as patient as they could be. But there wasn't much they could offer him. There were many others like him waiting for the same. Many, many more forms hovering around waiting for something, for anything. A little sympathy, a little kindness, a little understanding, a little more time to enjoy the luxury of owning a leg. Some were worse than him. But they gave him whatever they could spare of their time, their sympathy and their care. He had to make do with whatever they could give him. There

7

was no choice. Everything was in short supply. Including legs.

After many days a relative came to claim him, whatever was left of him. They had told his family that he was now able to leave. He was sent home. First in a wheelchair that made it up to the entrance of the hospital and from there he made do with a pair of sticks. The awkwardness of walking with sticks, the cushioned handles cutting deep into his armpits. He had to learn to live this way from now on. His stump was healing fast, yet there were hidden spaces that had not even started to heal. The missing pieces were yet to be understood. The shame of it all. The uselessness of his life.

He had lived for twenty two years and had hoped for three times more, but suddenly it all seemed too much. What would he do with all that time? The years seemed to stretch in front of him in an imaginary line that went on and on and on, with no end in sight. It all hit him hard like a hundred and one bullets against his chest. His breath caught in anguish. He wanted to cry, but his eyes were parched. He had run out of tears. It seemed that tears too were in short supply, just like legs. His soul had started to bleed, but no one seemed to have noticed this nor made an attempt to stem the flow. How could they, those who did not see, did not know?

The folks at home stood aghast when they saw him get out of the vehicle that had been hired to bring him home. They stared at him in horror as he strutted in through the door.

One leg.

Two sticks.

They didn't know what to do or how to react. They were embarrassed for him, for them. The silence grew. The pain continued to grow and grow like an unseen extension to his nonexistent leg. They spoke in whispers thinking the noise might disturb him. They had heard that loud noises might bring back the memories, the pain. So they did everything in silence, as much as they could. They were trying to be kind, to empathize as best they could, the only way they knew how.

They didn't realize it, but the silence cut deep into him, much deeper than the noise. The silence screamed out loud as a large bell, deafening him. He screamed out trying to block the silence, but it continued to grow and whisper. His family thought he was mad and reduced the volume of their speech even further. He screamed louder and the wind carried his unintelligible screams across the land. Yet no one cared. There were too many such people screaming to be heard. Their silent screams crisscrossed the length and breadth of the land and disappeared on the air. If someone heard him scream they merely ignored it as the screams of the crazed, just as his family did. His soul bled faster. He wanted to talk to his family, to cry out to them to treat him like they always did, but something stuck in his throat preventing the words from rushing out. They rose up in sentences, but the door to his lips held them back. They waited patiently for hours, then tired and returned to their source.

He sat on the cheap red plastic chair near the window and stared out at the garden. It was dried. The flowers wilted. The grass had turned brown in places where the sun scorched down on it. The wind roared overhead. The breezes blew harsh and hot against his skin. There was nothing that could please him. Not inside the house, not outside.

Inside the silence grew to an earth shattering scream; outside the ugliness rose to blind him. He heard his mother talking softly to the neighbor across the yellow and green croton fence separating the two compounds.

"We sent him to earn a living; to feed us, clothe us, build this house. He could have waited for at least a year. But look what the fool had to do. Now he's of no use to anyone."

# The Boarder

She blew herself up in the middle of traffic, taking with her everyone on the bus. She pulled on her strings like a bonbon at Christmas that snapped when pulled at the two ends revealing a treat inside. She revealed her true nature as she burst into flames inside the bus.

The people on the bus didn't know they would be accompanying her that evening as they journeyed home after work. Some children were making it home late after a long day at school followed by cricket practice for the upcoming match. Saliya was one of them. He knew Selvi who sat in the third row from the door. He had seen her around. Selvi was from Jaffna, or so she said. She kept to herself. Didn't speak to anyone, was somewhat polite to those she knew and didn't bother those she didn't know. He had never seen her smile at anyone either or acknowledge a known face, like a neighbor, as most of them did.

Maybe it was the language problem, Saliya thought. Selvi neither spoke Sinhala or English. Saliya wondered how she managed to get about, but the lack of knowledge of the language spoken in the area didn't appear to bother her.

Selvi came to live in Mrs. Kaluarachchi's house opposite Mr. Jinasena's shop. Mrs. Kaluarachchi ran a boarding house. She gave out rooms to girls who came to Colombo for studies or for jobs, and Selvi was one of them. They lived in her house as part of the family. There were three rooms in all. Seven girls stayed there, sharing the space. It was a little cramped, but no one complained. After all, it wasn't easy to find accommodation in the city. Housing was expensive and with the little money everyone seemed to be earning, it was amazing that one could even find a room in a shanty.

Everyone was migrating to the city for all kinds of reasons, but mainly for work. They earned enough to save a little and send some back home. But it was hard. Having a house in Colombo or a relative was a blessing that most people could only hope for. But it wasn't only those living in the rural areas that felt the pinch of the soaring cost of living. Folks in the city were burdened by it and more so than their brethren in the villages. The costs were higher and they didn't have a choice unlike their village brethren who could manage to get by with growing a few vegetables for their consumption in their very own gardens. But with the scarcity of land in the city this was merely a dream for most. Construction ruled. There were buildings everywhere. Offices, homes and shops. Those who were fortunate to have a big house resorted to partitioning a portion of it and renting it to families. Others, like Mrs. Kaluarachchi, brought in boarders.

Mrs. Kaluarachchi had been letting out her three rooms to boarders for the past twenty five years. She was fortunate she had the house that was passed down from her parents as a gift to her on her marriage. She didn't work, and her husband's salary was hardly enough to pay for their expenses. Their children needed to be taken care of – tuition fees, books, and other extras were paid for with the money Mrs. Kaluarachchi earned through letting her rooms out for strangers. She didn't mind cooking for them although at the beginning it had been hard. But she had got used to it and knew how to manage as best she could. After ten years she got a woman to come help her with the cooking and this made things easier.

Selvi came to stay with the Kaluarachchi's about two years ago. Mrs. Kaluarachchi had not been happy about taking a Tamil girl in, what with the trouble and all that, but Selvi's brother had pleaded, saying they really needed the money as things were hard in Jaffna. It was the same old story: Selvi's father had been killed by the LTTE because he didn't have the money ready when they came, or so it was said. He had been paying the Tamil terrorists faithfully every month, but he could not work for three months after he met with the accident and it was hard to feed the family.

Narendran, the son did odd jobs for the army stationed in the area and the family managed to get by with that money. But there wasn't enough when the LTTE's representative came calling. Selvi's father had been stalling payment for three months, and every time the old man pleaded with the representative to spare them until he was able to get up and return to work. On that fateful day it was a different representative that came calling. He wasn't interested in the old man's pleas. Just give us the money was all he said. The old man opened his mouth to plead, and that was when the bullet entered his brain: through his open mouth, cutting through into his brain. He fell dead immediately and it was only when his wife began to scream that anyone knew what had happened. It had been so sudden.

After the funeral Narendran had taken over the responsibilities. He had just finished school and was awaiting entry into university. Selvi was the eldest. She had finished university a year before Narendran and was already looking out for a job. They all agreed that she would come to Colombo to work until Narendran finished his degree and started work to support the younger siblings and their ailing mother.

Someone they knew in Jaffna had spoken to a friend running a NGO in Colombo and suggested that Selvi work there for some time. It would be good to get some experience, and who knows, she might even get the opportunity to go abroad, the old friend had said. Most people in the NGOs were sympathetic to the Tamils and would help them in any way they could, he said. So she came to Colombo, or so she told everyone.

☙ ☙ ☙

Selvi started work a week ago, but she still didn't have a proper place to stay. The Guest House they were lodged at was too expensive and one of the inmates suggested she stay in a boarding in the suburbs as it was cheaper. Also it was safe as most boarding house owners were strict about who came and went. Selvi and Narendran heard about Mrs. Kaluarachchi through someone else and came to visit her.

"Please madam," Narendran said. "Please let my sister stay with you. I promise she will not bother you or give you any trouble."

Selvi nodded and bowed her head. Mrs. Kaluarachchi being the kindly person felt pity on the girl. So far away from home and her family. Not speaking the language and not knowing a soul. Her heart softened. She agreed to take her in against her better judgment.

"After all," she told her husband, "We can't be living in suspicion of all Tamils can we? They are also having a hard time just like us."

Her husband merely grunted and didn't say anything. Mrs. Kaluarachchi had been running the boarding meticulously and except for one incident involving one of the girls at about the time they started running the boarding there were never any trouble with any of the boarders. They were all from good families and all they wanted was a safe place to stay in Colombo until they completed their studies. Some were university students, others came in for work and stayed on until they married and left to set up home with their husbands, or they would remain in the boarding until they had earned enough money to rent out a small flat. Still, it was the first time they had let in a Tamil girl, and Mr. Kaluarachchi was a little apprehensive.

"We don't know anything about her," he said, lines of anxiety creasing his brow.

"Yes, we don't. But we could find out, can't we? She works at some NGO and a family acquaintance is known to one of the directors there. That's how she came to work there. She can't be a bad person," Mrs. Kaluarachchi replied.

"I'm not suggesting she's a bad person. But one can never say what they are up to, can we? In this day and age with all the trouble the LTTE is creating we have to be careful, not only for ourselves but those around us. How can we put everyone else here at risk?" Mr. Kaluarachchi asked.

"I will keep an eye on her, and if she behaves suspiciously I will ask her to leave," Mrs. Kaluarachchi assured.

Mr. Kaluarachchi sighed and picked up the papers. His wife did have a point. One couldn't be suspicious of all the Tamil people. They couldn't all be supporters of the LTTE. But he was nevertheless concerned. There was the children's safety as well as the safety of the other boarders.

"How will she manage here without any knowledge of the language?" he asked suddenly.

His wife looked at him for a moment before responding.

"She seems to understand a little English and I think as time goes by she will learn some Sinhala words, at least enough to get by. Nalika knows a little Tamil and she can help her as well."

"Nalika knows Tamil? I never knew that!" Mr. Kaluarachchi sounded amazed.

"Yes, she had taken a course in basic Tamil while waiting to enter university."

Nalika was one of the boarders who had been staying with the Kaluarachchis for over five years. Her parents were from Ambalangoda, in the south, and were known to the Kaluarachchis. When Nalika was selected to university it was a foregone conclusion that she would stay with the Kaluarachchis although it was a little far from the

17

university she would be studying at. But that was alright. It was better to stay with known people than total strangers even if it meant travelling a little further a little longer each day.

"I wonder why she didn't stay with Tamil people but thought of coming here," Mr. Kaluarachchi mused.

"Yes, I wondered too. Maybe there wasn't room with any of the Tamils keeping boarders," his wife reasoned.

"But surely, they could have found some place? She is totally among strangers here. At least with a Tamil family she would be able to speak the same language and eat the same food."

"Yes it's true. She could also have stayed with the Muslims running the boardings too? They also speak Tamil, and things would have been much easier for Selvi. I wonder why she decided to come and stay with us, and so far away from the usual Tamil areas too," Mrs. Kaluarachchi said, a note of trepidation entering her voice.

But she didn't voice her growing concern lest it upset her husband more than he already seemed to be. She vowed to keep a close watch on Selvi to see how she was getting on. It wouldn't do if she became lonely or homesick. How would they know what she was going through if they couldn't communicate? Mrs. Kaluarachchi felt a wave of pity for the girl. At least Nalika is there for her if she needs anything, she consoled herself.

The police were as concerned as the Kaluarachchis were. But their concern was more to do with security than with the language problem that Mrs. Kaluarachchi was concerned with.

"Do you have any idea who she is?" the officer taking down Selvi's details asked Mr. Kaluarachchi.

Usually Mrs. Kaluarachchi accompanied the girls who came to stay in the boarding to the police station for registering. It was a requirement that all those living in any house for more than a few days be registered with the police in the area. It was for national security reasons and no one complained as they were all concerned about their safety too. Selvi had brought several letters with her, one from the director of the NGO she worked at, one from the police post near her home, and one from the acquaintance who recommended her for the job in Colombo. All these she left with the police along with a copy of her National Identity Card. Everything appeared to be in order and the police officer didn't ask any further questions. The Kaluarachchis were respectable people in the area and never troubled anyone. They were known to take very good care of the girls that stayed in their home. There was never a complaint from anyone. Once a female officer attached to the police had also stayed there and had nothing but praise for the way she was treated. But like Mr. Kaluarachchi, the police officer too couldn't understand why a Tamil girl would want to stay with a Sinhala family in a predominantly Sinhala area.

"Maybe they thought she would be safer among the Sinhalese as the family was threatened by the LTTE. Living away from any Tamil speaking person could prevent anyone from threatening her further, or trying to extort money from her," Mr. Kaluarachchi reasoned.

"Yes, that could be so," the police officer replied.

"There is a lot of trouble among the Tamil people even here," the police officer at the next table said. "We have heard of the police in Wellawatte having to break up fights between gangs trying to extort money from innocent civilians who have come to Colombo for whatever reason."

"It's as if they can't be free from the LTTE's clutches anywhere they go."

"Yes, even when they go abroad there will be someone following them for money."

"What a life. Maybe this one wanted some peace." He looked kindly at the girl. "Her father was killed in front of her eyes, you said."

"Yes. That's what the brother said. Shot through the head when he tried to protest. It must have been traumatic," Mr. Kaluarachchi said.

"There are so many such cases it has almost become normal. Some of our colleagues serving in police stations in the troubled areas tell us things we can only imagine. It's like things you sometimes see on TV. Not real. But it is so real. It really is sad. Those Tamil terrorists are only interested in destroying this country and they don't seem to care if they kill their own people as long as they get what they want."

Saliya watched her sitting quietly at the front. He had never spoken to her although she lived a few houses from his own. He would see her returning home from work every day while he and his friends played cricket on the road. She never looked at anyone but looked through them. Never smiled. It was as if she didn't know how to smile. In all those months of seeing her, not once had she acknowledged the presence of any one of her neighbors or those standing at the bus stop. People smiled at least after seeing another face more than a couple of times and although they might not speak as everyone was busy rushing someplace, there would always be time for a smile as they passed, or an acknowledging nod of the head. But Selvi looked through everyone as she walked on the road. If she went to a shop to buy something she would not speak to anyone either, but get her things, pay the money and leave. Even on the bus she never said a word, but gave the exact change and received her ticket to her destination.

It wasn't only because of the language problem. She could converse a little in Sinhala and English, but she didn't bother to try and strike up a conversation with anyone. Even Nalika had been somewhat taken aback by Selvi's rudeness and disinterest at Nalika's attempts to help her. Nalika had taught her a few Sinhala words as she had asked, but soon after mastering the words and the sentences required to get about the place Selvi dropped her friendly demeanor and resumed her old nature. No one could understand why she refused to take the offers of friendship. It was as if she had a ball of hate inside her that refused to let her be friends with those trying to make friends with her. But they tried all the same and continued to do so. Mrs. Kaluarachchi the most.

Saliya felt sorry for Mrs. Kaluarachchi. She was a really nice woman who always had a kind word for everyone. Sometimes she would call in the boys playing cricket on the road and offer them sandwiches or some sweets she had made. Selvi sat in front of the bus as if she didn't care.

22

Saliya's friends were talking and joking among themselves. It had been a good game, but they were all tired. It was a happy sense of tiredness; the kind felt when everything was going alright. The bus was crowded as it was the evening rush hour. Everyone was sitting or standing close like sardines inside a tin. The body smells were all over and it was fortunate there was no rain and the windows could be kept open to let in the cool evening breeze. But with the bumper to bumper traffic there was not a breath of air coming through.

Everyone waited. There was nothing else to do in a traffic jam. Then two off-duty police officers got into the bus. They stood at the footboard in front talking to the driver and exchanging pleasantries. Saliya saw Selvi sit up as the policemen entered. She seemed to be nervous. It was the first time he had seen her show any sign of life ever and he was immediately alert. The policemen didn't notice anything as they stood in front of the bus talking. They too were like the other people on the bus trying to get home after a long day at work. One of them looked back at the sound of a woman complaining loudly about someone stepping on her foot. Selvi shifted nervously in her seat as the policeman glanced back.

The woman's voice rose as it seemed the man who stepped on her foot had either stepped on it again or had refused to apologize. The man's voice could be heard too. An injured tone as if he had done nothing and the woman was singling him out for something he was not responsible for. The policeman called out to the back, trying to help. The woman's voice rose higher in protest. Selvi picked up her bag and pushed against the person standing next to her. He didn't move as the surge from the crowd pushed him further towards the space between the two seats.

"Wait until the bus stops at the bus stop, then the crowd will ease," he motioned to Selvi thinking she was trying to get up to get off the bus.

The policeman tried to make his way towards the place where he heard the voice from. He had just reached the front seat when Selvi stood up. Everyone froze as she let out a loud cry like an animal and lifted her arms above her head. There was a flash of bright light and then a loud noise like nothing they had heard.

ॐ ॐ ॐ

Mrs. Kaluarachchi was getting worried. It was almost seven thirty and Selvi had not returned as yet. It was not like her. She always returned before six. Whatever could have happened to make her get so late? Mrs. Kaluarachchi walked outside and stood at the gate watching the people trickle

24

past the house or stop in front of Mr. Jinasena's shop to buy something.

"Why Mrs. Perera, what's the matter?" Mrs. Kaluarachchi asked seeing her neighbor standing in front of the shop, a strange look on her face.

"My son hasn't returned yet," Mrs. Perera sighed heavily and then added weakly, "they just said that a bomb has gone off in Colombo."

Mr. Jinasena came out from inside the shop.

"They didn't say much over the radio. Maybe they'll give more details for the news," he said and stared out in front of him. "None of the other boys have returned either," he added with a grave look on his face.

"Maybe it's the traffic," Mrs. Kaluarachchi said soothingly, trying to console her neighbor. "It's rush hour and if one gets caught up in that traffic then there are no guarantees of returning early. Selvi is late too. She is never late. It must be the traffic," she said as if to reassure herself.

"Oh I hope it's just the traffic. You never know these days, what with all those bombs going off all over the place," Mrs. Perera shuddered.

"Don't even think such things. It's probably the traffic," Mrs. Kaluarachchi exclaimed in horror but her heart was straining and she could barely stand.

What if Selvi had got caught to the bomb? She thought and shuddered. What would she tell Selvi's family?

"Yes, I suppose you are right," Mrs. Perera said and sighed. "It's probably the traffic."

Mrs. Kaluarachchi closed the gate and walked slowly to the house. Her mind was in turmoil as she grappled with the facts she had just heard. Her husband was sitting on the verandah.

"The boys down the road haven't returned either," she said sounding worried "I was just speaking to Mrs. Perera. Her son and the other boys had stayed back from school for cricket practice. They haven't returned yet. She was standing near Jinasena's shop," Mrs. Kaluarachchi said as she sat down.

She stared in front of her for a while and then continued.

"Mrs. Perera was worried because there was a bomb blast in Colombo" she said trying to sound unconcerned.

Her husband looked at her strangely.

"Yes, I heard something like that on the radio just now," he said slowly.

Mrs. Kaluarachchi turned to look at him.

"Are you sure?" she whispered. "No it can't be. I hope nothing has happened to Selvi," she placed her hand on her chest and stared at her husband. "Did they say where in Colombo? Was it close to this side?" but Mr. Kaluarachchi didn't seem to know.

Later that night the Kaluarachchis watched as the images of the carnage caused by the bomb blast flashed across the television screen. It had happened somewhere along the Galle Road in Wellawatte, not so far away. There were many deaths. It was rush hour traffic and the bus was packed.

"Do you think they were anywhere near that?" she asked hesitantly.

"You mean those boys?" her husband asked not taking his eyes off the screen.

Yes," she murmured looking worried. "What if those bats they just showed belonged to those boys?" she almost wailed.

Nalika and the other three girls were also worried, but they didn't say anything lest it upset Mrs. Kaluarachchi more. It was now past nine and there was no sign of Selvi. After a while Mrs. Kaluarachchi spoke,

"should we try to find out where Selvi is?"

"How?" her husband asked. "We don't know any of her friends. Does she even have any friends?" he turned towards Nalika.

"I don't know. Maybe she has friends at the office," Nalika said rather doubtfully.

"Do you know anyone at her office?" Mr. Kaluarachchi asked.

Nalika shook her head to indicate the negative.

"You know she doesn't tell us anything," Nalika said. "And she doesn't seem to get any letters from home or friends. She doesn't keep any photographs either. There's nothing personal."

"We could call the office and find out," Mrs. Kaluarachchi said switching off the television.

"At this time? There won't be anyone now. We will have to wait until tomorrow," Mr. Kaluarachchi said.

"Should we inform the police?" Mrs. Kaluarachchi asked after a while still sounding worried.

"Whatever for?" her husband wanted to know. "Haven't they got enough of work trying to catch thieves without having to now go looking for a missing person that we don't know is missing for sure? For all you know she must be working late. Or maybe she went to visit a friend," Mr. Kaluarachchi said. "Besides the police will not accept a

28

complaint of a missing person until forty eight hours have passed. We will just have to wait and see."

Then seeing the look on his wife's face he added,

"she must have gone to see a friend and forgot to inform us."

But Mrs. Kaluarachchi was beginning to have doubts about that. She resigned herself to the fate that she would face in the coming days that someone would call and tell her that Selvi too had been an unfortunate victim that lost out to the terror of the times. How would she break the news to Selvi's brother? She kept repeating over and over to herself. What could she say to that family that had lost a father, and now a daughter?

The newspapers the next day had more news than the television the previous night. Mrs. Kaluarachchi picked up the paper and stared at it. There were many pictures of the bomb site. There was also a new picture they hadn't shown on the television; a large picture on the front page with the news that the police were seeking information about someone that looked a lot like Selvi in connection with the blast. They had found the head of a woman against the side of a ditch and this was the head of the terrorist, or so the police said. It was the picture of that head that stared out at her from the papers.

Mrs. Kaluarachchi gasped out loud and sank into the chair on the verandah. She could not speak. It was as if the breath was caught inside her refusing to come out. Could this be true? Had she misjudged? The thought that she might have contributed to this in a small way stunned her further. She just sat there tears welling in her eyes.

# Man from the East

Every time Aruni left the house she would take a good look at every man she saw. Was he the one? She asked herself every time, and each time she answered it immediately with an emphatic no. Where would we meet she wondered. Would it be someone I know or a complete stranger? Would he come home or should I have to find him someplace else? These were the thoughts running through her mind. She was surprised that she had become so obsessed with the idea of a man who would come from a particular direction and sweep her off her feet. Or would he merely ask her? After all, the sweeping part was reserved only for characters in fairy tales and she was no character in a fairy tale.

Aruni had not spent much time in brooding over the lack of a husband or the need to find someone soon. She had gone through the process of meeting supposedly suitable men only to find their suitability wanting in many areas. She had tired of the whole process and decided not to go looking for anyone. It was too much of a bother. Besides where was one to look? She was happy the way things were. She was single, yes, and most of the relatives on her conservative father's side were very unhappy that she wasn't married as yet.

"It is high time she got married, don't you think?" she heard her paternal aunt telling her mother when she came visiting one day.

That was five years ago. They hadn't seen the aunt since and Aruni was sure she would have the same question ready to pop out at the least provocation if ever they saw her again.

It was a major calamity, no less in significance than a landslide or a flood, to be unmarried after a certain age. And it wasn't just the relatives who stirred the fires and kept the idea running, neighbors and distant friends added fuel. It was as if all of society expected everyone to be married. Or else.

There was a certain way people looked at women who were unmarried. As if they were rejects of society. People who had not made an effort to walk at the normal pace and had therefore missed the bus. They had missed the second bus and the third and the fourth until none of the busses were interested in stopping, or they made no attempt to flag down a bus, but waited at the bus stop for a nonexistent bus. This same attitude was not passed onto single men. There didn't seem to be anything amiss in a man not getting married. No one commented on it. But an unmarried woman. There must be something wrong.

"Your daughter is still not married?" Mrs. Gunawardene shrilled out at Aruni's mother when they met on the road.

She was returning home after visiting a friend, and they were off to town to catch a bus to visit friends.

"No, not yet," Aruni's mother replied and tried to move on but Mrs. Gunawardene had all the time in the world to gossip and wasn't willing to let go of a juicy subject like an unmarried daughter.

"My grand-daughter got married last year," she burst out, a satisfied look on her fat wrinkled face. "She married the local government agent's son. They are very well off now. They live in government quarters. I just visited them last week."

The satisfied look on her face spread to her neck. The wrinkles around her neck jingled their fat like heavy gold chains. It coursed down the too-full-of-fat-arms to settle on her gnarled old fingertips. She lifted her right hand and patted a stray hair that had fallen across her face back onto her head. The satisfaction entered her hair follicles and they swayed cockishly in the cool breeze that blew their way just then.

"That is good. You must be very happy," Aruni's mother said, and made as if to move on.

"Yes, yes. And now she is expecting a child."

The satisfaction could not hold itself any longer. It burst through every pore of her body and hovered about her, dancing like flies near a two week old dustbin.

"We have to go," Aruni's mother said, finally trying to break free of Mrs. Gunewardene's invisible tentacles.

Mrs. Gunewardene's face fell but the sagging flesh on her neck managed to push it back up. She couldn't hide her disappointment.

"Why so soon..." she wailed.

She had not been able to get any information, so keen was she on spreading her good news that she had not bothered to ask any questions. She looked Aruni up and down and let them pass. It was not a nice look. It was a look that said you are pathetic, a reject, no one wants you, you are an aberration of society.

Mrs. Gunewardene always gave people that look. It was a special look she had prepared for all women who were considered, by her standards and view to be unworthy. If they were unmarried the look deepened, if they were married she'd inquire about their husbands, the work they did, the position they held and who their relatives were. Then she would harrumph her discontent and look them up and down, up and down several times before proceeding to inform them about the families her children had married into. Not that it made any difference to anyone listening.

Her relatives were as much nobodies to others as they were somebodies to her.

It was the same look she had given Aruni's grandmother so many years ago when Aruni's grandmother was looking for men for her daughters. She had stopped by the gate to speak to her grandmother in the garden to comment on her good fortune at having married off all her six daughters and two sons while Aruni's grandmother, several years her senior had not managed to get even one daughter engaged. According to Mrs. Gunewardene, if a girl was married but had not produced a single child within the space of two years, there was something very wrong with her. Then Mrs. Gunewardene reached her zenith. She would practically crow with delight about it to everyone she saw, anywhere.

Aruni despised Mrs. Gunewardene and people like her. She tried to avoid them as much as she could, but it was hard to ignore them when they accosted her on the street. There was really nothing wrong in being unmarried. Times had changed and women were working and earning their own living. They were able to take care of themselves financially and didn't have to be dependent on a husband for their wellbeing unlike the women of her grandmother's generation. But things had conspired to change her thinking process. She did not give a second glance to men passing by her on the street, in the supermarket or restaurant, but since lately she had started looking at every man with some degree of interest. Even the ugly fellow with betel-stained red lips that came asking for work the previous week. Although she found him extremely ugly and disgusting she found herself wondering if he lived in the eastern direction. Aruni shuddered at the way her thinking had gone. How could she have sunk so low in her expectations, and within such a short space of time? She was also a little amused. Here was her mind playing with the little germ planted there. And it was all because they had visited the astrologer.

"A suitable man will come from the East. He will not come looking for marriage at first, but will meet you, maybe as a friend or acquaintance. He will later come with a proposal for marriage. Don't be hasty. But be careful in deciding. Do you understand what I'm saying?"

He peered at Aruni with a gentle smile on his gnarled old face and waited for her answer.

"Yes," Aruni said.

She was sitting in the chair in front of the old man who was reading her horoscope.

"What type of person is he?" Aruni's mother inquired impatiently.

"He is from a very good family. Very wealthy and good qualities. But here's what you should be careful about."

He peered at Aruni as if to check if he had her full attention.

"He should be residing in the Eastern direction from where you reside. Do you understand? Do not agree to anything else as it won't be right. He has to be from the East," he said emphatically, sat back after that pronouncement, and waited for their questions.

They had gone to see the old man because someone said he was good. Unlike most of the other astrologers who had no idea what they were saying, but said something just for the sake of it, just to please whoever came to get their futures read. This one was an old man, very religious, who didn't charge a lot for the reading. He was a genuine person, they were informed. He wouldn't say the type of nonsense the others usually said just to please. So they had gone to see him.

"Shaa! This is a very good horoscope. Very good," the old man wheezed when they sat down and gave him the horoscope.

He squinted at the writings on the long strip of ola then looked at Aruni as if to get a response. He found none, so he continued to gush.

"There's absolutely nothing to worry about. Nothing," he added, and waited for a response.

Seeing there was no response forthcoming he continued,

"Was there something in particular you wanted to know?" he inquired.

He seemed genuinely perplexed as to why they had come to him.

"Nothing seems to be going right," Aruni's mother grumbled from the side. "She can't get a proper job and there is a lot of opposition to everything she tries to do."

"That's because Saturn is ruling" he exclaimed as if everyone was expected to know this. "What do you expect? That fellow doesn't allow anything to happen. He tries to prevent it. That is why everything she has done has not had any benefit," he said with disgust, then peered through his bushy eyebrows falling like dreadlocks across his eyes and smiled. "But you don't have to worry anymore. Saturn is going away. His time is limited. He has only a few more months left. And then he is gone. You will not see him again for,"

And there he stopped to leaf through a book he had with a timetable of the arrivals and departures of various planets. He found the page he was looking for and studied it for a moment before responding.

"...fifteen years. He will be gone for fifteen years," he said and closed the book. "You have fifteen years of good fortune," he said, stepping out of the room.

He went towards the nearest plant at the edge of the compound wall and spat out onto the ground near the plant.

"I have a very bad cough," he said on returning, and sat down.

He cleared his throat several times as if to emphasize the seriousness of his cough and picked up the ola strip again.

"What does your husband do?" he asked looking through his dreadlocks at Aruni.

"I don't have a husband," she replied.

"What? You aren't married?" he bellowed almost falling over his chair.

"No," she replied.

"But it says here that you should be married by now. How old did you say you were?" he asked sounding perplexed.

"Thirty seven," Aruni replied.

"That's not possible." He sounded stunned.

"Nothing came right," Aruni's mother said.

"Was there no one interested in her?" He looked at Aruni's mother inquiringly.

"There were a few, but nothing came of it," she replied again.

"Saturn again," he exclaimed, and looked as if he would like to wring Saturn's neck that very minute.

Aruni and her mother exchanged glances. He looked at them pensively for a moment, then held up the ola again. After satisfying himself with the contents of the writing on the ola he took up another arrivals and departures schedule for the planets.

"We must do something about this. She should be married by this time."

He stopped his study of the timetable to smile at Aruni.

"Don't worry, my dear. We will make things right. As long as there is life in these old bones of mine you have nothing to worry. Eh?"

He smiled at Aruni like she was a long lost relative.

"What can we do?" Aruni's mother asked.

"Are you Buddhist?" he asked peering at her from under his dreadlocks.

"Yes," Aruni's mother replied.

"Then do a lot of Bodhi pooja. Give alms to the poor," he said. "There are a couple of months left of Saturn. You should feed the crows. That is a very good thing to do. The crow is Saturn's vehicle. He is always hungry."

He put down the departure schedule and looked into the distance a slightly sorrowful look on his face as if he was experiencing the hunger of the crows.

"Did you know that the crow doesn't have a proper digestive tract like other birds? Everything it eats remains only as long as it enters its body and leaves. That is why crows are always hungry. It is very meritorious to feed a being like that. You should dip pieces of cloth in ghee and give it to the crows with some rice. You can use the cloth wicks used to light oil lamps for this."

He looked at the calendar on the wall.

"Today is Tuesday."

"No, it's Wednesday," Aruni interrupted.

"You are so right. It is Wednesday. Whatever happened to Tuesday?" he looked out of the window as if he expected Tuesday to enter that very minute and answer his question.

He sighed.

"How the time flies. Here was I thinking it was Tuesday and yesterday was Monday. What was I doing yesterday? Tuesday, Tuesday..." he stared at the wall lost in thought, one hand still holding the ola and the other on his chin.

"Right!" he suddenly exclaimed, coming out of reverie. "If you start this Saturday it will be good. Saturday is Saturn's day, so Saturn will also be happy," he said and smiled his toothy smile.

"Should we start the Bodhi pooja on Saturday as well?" Aruni's mother asked.

"No no. Not necessary. You can start the Bodhi pooja any day. Even today. It would be better if you go to the temple, but if there is no temple close to your home, you can chant at home," he said.

"There is a temple close by. We can go there," Aruni's mother said.

"Then what is the problem?"

He seemed satisfied.

"Now for a husband."

He looked at Aruni.

"According to your horoscope you should have been married already. But you are not. Maybe some previous bad karma took effect and prevented this from happening. If you do good things you will have positive benefits. Keep doing Bodhi pooja and feeding the less fortunate. That is a very meritorious thing to do."

He sat back in his armchair and sighed.

It had been a month since Saturn took flight to another direction. That was as per the departure schedule of the old man. Aruni had fed the crows, done the Bodhi pooja and given alms to the Bhikkhus in the temple as well as prepared lunch packets for the old beggars in the town. She had stopped thinking of the man from the East. She couldn't care less. The original interest had waned with the passing of time and the non arrival of the mysterious easterner had been replaced with the get-together her friends were planning for the end of the month.

"Did he say house or town?" Nilusha, her cousin asked.

She was also curious about the man and was waiting to see if things turned out as planned for Aruni to go consult the old man.

"What does it matter if it is house or town? He said place where I live," Aruni said, an amused look on her face.

"So? Place where you live could be both town and home, couldn't it? You need to be more specific. If it is town then the direction is that way," Nilusha said gesturing, "but if it is house, it is in that direction." she pointed to another direction. "What will you do?"

"He has to first come, hasn't he? And then he has to show interest," Aruni replied.

43

"Forget all this nonsense. Things don't happen like that. Men don't appear like that out of the blues," Aruni's mother said. "You will become chronic thinking about it like that."

"Yes, don't do that. See what happened to us. Some astrologer said something and your grandmother jumped at it. We spent our youth being miserable and waiting for any man to come and take us," Nilusha's mother replied.

The two girls exchanged tired looks. Their mothers always brought up the subject of their unmarried–status-problems during their youth and their grandmothers' efforts to get them married. Samanthi and Chamari, Aruni's school - friends grinned at them. They lived in the next town and had dropped in for a chat. Their mothers were no different from Aruni's and Nilusha's. When the conversation turned to marriage it seemed all women with unmarried daughters had the same thing to say.

"Maybe he's not coming because he's busy," Samanthi offered, a wicked grin on her face.

"Yes, maybe he got held up with some important project," Nilusha added. "Or maybe the bus he was traveling in broke down."

"Chee, he travels by bus!" Aruni exclaimed in mock horror. "The astrologer said he was very wealthy, so what happened to all the wealth? Couldn't he at least have spared some to buy a car?" she demanded.

"Maybe he lost all his wealth on the way and had to take a bus," Chamari said dryly.

"Didn't you say he had to come from the East? Maybe the roads are closed."

That was Samanthi.

"Yes, maybe he's stuck in Thoppigala fighting for his life and can't even think of coming over," said Nilusha.

"Maybe he's risking his life on the battlefield just to impress you," said Chamari. "Just imagine that. How chivalrous!"

"You mean to say he's in the army?" Aruni asked.

"Maybe," Chamari replied.

"Or maybe he's a Tiger," Samanthi offered.

"Aiyooooh, no, no," Aruni's mother wailed from the next room. "Don't even think of that."

"Maybe he's been caught by the army and is sitting inside an iron cage waiting for Aruni to come and let him out," Samanthi continued, loud enough for Aruni's mother to hear, a wicked grin on her face.

"You girls are so ridiculous," Aruni's mother said, coming to stand at the door.

"But that's what the man said. You were there," Aruni said.

Her mother glared at her and was about to leave the room when Samanthi spoke.

"How can a planet as large as Saturn travel on the back of a crow?" she asked.

"What nonsense are you talking about?" Nilusha's mother asked joining the group inside Aruni's room.

"The astrologer said the crow was Saturn's vehicle and we should feed the crows because of this," Aruni replied.

"If you go to believe everything everyone says you will end up a mental wreck," Aruni's mother said.

"Yes. Just forget about it," Nilusha's mother consoled.

"What's the vehicle of the planet that's ruling right now?" Nilusha asked.

"I have no idea. What is its vehicle?" Aruni asked, and they both looked at their respective mothers.

"What's the ruling planet?" Chamari asked.

"I really don't remember," Nilusha's mother said.

"Then why bother what the vehicle is?" Chamari offered.

"We could leave some food out for it if we knew," Aruni said.

"And how would you call out to it if it's a caterpillar?" questioned Samanthi curiously.

"I have no idea. Maybe I'll call 'kaak, kaak,'" Aruni replied.

"But that's for a crow!" Chamari exclaimed.

"So? Why can't a caterpillar respond?" asked Aruni.

"No one would have a caterpillar for a vehicle. It's too tiny," Nilusha concluded.

"Yeah, right. Then how do you explain the elephant god traveling on the rat?" Chamari asked.

"Oh keep quiet all of you," Aruni's mother said and walked towards the kitchen.

"So what do we do about the man?" Nilusha asked.

"Don't tell me you still believe that ridiculous old man?" Aruni exclaimed, surprised that her cousin was so serious about it.

"Maybe Saturn took your husband away with him. That's why he is not coming," Samanthi offered.

"You mean to say he's a driver?" Aruni asked. "Aiyoh, what a thing."

"Maybe your husband is Saturn's vehicle and since Saturn needs a ride your husband had no choice but to oblige the planet. Even if he didn't want to," Chamari said.

"If he was a vehicle I wonder what type he would be, a Mercedes or a plain dull Maruti?" Aruni mused.

Chamari grinned.

"Can you believe how low he has sunk?"

"I quite like that concept. So the man has to do vehicle duty for Saturn and can't come to Aruni because he's tied up," Samanthi added.

"I think you're right. So now we have to wait until Saturn returns," Nilusha said.

"When does Saturn return?" Chamari asked.

"In fifteen years...That's according to the astrologer," Aruni replied.

"Oh my, forgot it. You'll be an old cow by the time he returns," Samanthi said.

"I really think you should find someone else. Why don't we try looking for someone from the West?" Nilusha offered.

"Yes, that's a better idea. Check the newspapers. Maybe there's something about someone coming from America. That's in the West right?" Chamari said.

"You are all quite mad," Nilusha's mother said rather annoyed, and walked out of the room.

# Emerald Silk

She watched the green leaves on the branch outside the window turn dark against the drops of water that soaked into them, wiping the leaves clean from the turbulence of the mundane dust that endeavored to cloak them from the sun. The water washed away the years of dust that perched on the leaves, falling in droplets against other leaves washing them too and finally collected in their own engineered droplets against the soft, damp earth below. The leaves turned dark and clean and sparkled like the emerald silk dress she wore two months ago when he left; the day he walked out after their words, banging the door shut annoyed with her response; the day she left him and that cold, unfeeling prison never to return again although she did not tell him this at that time. Do not tell this to him even now as she sat watching the water on the leaves outside falling, falling, washing, washing leaf by leaf. The leaves clean in their original splendor reminded her of herself on that night they parted. Her mind drifted back to words spoken, phrases recanted, yet her mind didn't react to thoughts of the past. It was too numb. Or was it just the shock of realization that numbed?

The rain washed away the dust of centuries, turning everything it touched anew. That was the way of the rain. A fresh street, a clean tree or fresh hope for better things to come. Yet it couldn't wash away her thoughts, her past or her indecisions that lay like dormant serpents coiled against the cool, hard weave of a coir basket that entombed them to a life of darkness. It wouldn't be able to wash them away even if she stood with her head to the wind, her eyes raised up to take in the water as it fell into her eyes and seeped into her body to wash away her thoughts of him and his life.

Her thoughts could never be washed clean. They were like the serpents lying inside their basket to emerge only when desired, demanded. Never set free. Never able to be set free lest they harmed someone by their reckless lust for freedom. They lay there in hopeful anticipation of the day when all hell broke loose and the fetters of servitude were thrown to the wind. But until then they lay strewn, strained and dejected.

How would this all end? He was there in that cold, hard prison hedged in by concrete and cocooned by grey clouds, while she was out here gazing from her window upon wet, green leaves the color of her emerald silk dress, thinking of him in that cold, damp, undignified dump he called a home.

He lived in a place no less similar to a cardboard box. He called it his home and expected her to creep in with him; to snuff out her dreams of a future, to share the cramped existence he called life. Her back ached with the memory of crawling through the endless compartments he called rooms to finally lay flat on her aching back, exhausted. Only for a few hours and then the bliss was interrupted by the ringing of the doorbell signaling the entry of the world into those cramped circumstances of a home. And she was forced to get up and smile her tears away. They talked about the beast living inside a box. How modern, how defined. Yet her eyes screamed for the traditional, for the usual that he rejected in his quest for the modern, not really knowing what he was seeking. He interpreted her screams as a high for the beauty of that existence. His existence. Never hers.

She made up her mind. It was what was best. That evening she took out the emerald silk. No one wore emerald silk in that modern space of emerald earth that had been turned concrete grey. It was undefined, aged and decadent. But she was defiant. She wore her emerald silk that reminded her of the leaves on the branch that beat against the open window panes of her bedroom, laughing in the breeze, streaks of sunlight flitting from one leaf to another, or heavy with unsoaked rain. And she made up her mind. The emerald silk cocooned her, bringing in familiarity and a sense of belonging to the earth and all it held. She gained sustenance to stand up on faltering feet.

This was the end. The last dance of fantasy was in motion. She walked out of the cardboard box home with her head held up high. Her back ached, but she knew it was the end. Her life with him had ended. His was a life led one trillion light years away. His life was defined the moment he was born. He willed himself to be conditioned to live inside a box close to the sky, away from the earth and all it held. He lived in the clouds and looked down at the world below, not really understanding what it all meant. Her life was different from his, up there in the cloud. That was no life for her. Heights made her dizzy. She fell into the abyss of her undefined dreams and emerald silk.

But how would she ever tell him that she would not return to him? The distance widened as he waited in anticipation. She would not be drawn in ever again into the vortex of his dejection. She needed to find the words to tell him that she would not be drawn again into that sallow cardboard box of his home. How would she ever tell him she wouldn't return? What could she possibly say to make him understand that hers was a life that was better, fuller and more colored, while all he represented was dullness and drudgery?

She counted the raindrops falling on to the leaves. They slid down to land on the moist grass standing up to attention with its tiny leaves reaching out to the sky, glad for all it was offered. They slithered through the heavy weave of the grass to mingle and run into the brown earth below, only to make its way through little streams underground to travel down, down, down, to emerge in rivers that ran to the sea, then up into the sky and back again on to emerald green. She watched the raindrops falling, falling for what seemed like a lifetime. Then she climbed out of the window and joined the raindrops.

Like the grass, she lifted up her head to the sky and felt the raindrops caress her face, her arms, her hair. She flowed, she ran, now deep in the earth, now sparkling in the sun held afloat by trillions of laughing, laughing raindrops growing salty. She soared, free as the wind that held her afloat. She was finally at peace with herself. At peace with the memory of him inside his cardboard house. Free once more to be a raindrop if she chose. She was once again herself. She rose and fell and rose again. The chains that held her down were lost in the dust of his imagination. She soared.

# Photographs in Her Mind

Engamma was old with fear. The expression of terror on the faces of her two young sons being dragged out of her house as she watched helpless flashed across her mind like a screensaver on her daughter's computer. It flashed all the time: when she was sitting alone inside her home staring at the wall in front of her or the tree in the garden or when she was stirring the curry on the fire – their little faces would appear on the surface of the gravy startling her and carrying her back to that day so many years ago. It never seemed like it was so long ago although it had been over twenty years. The images were as new as if they had taken place that very morning. Engamma was cursed with the memory that would never leave. While others forgot as time moved on or the images dulled and dimmed like the spots and marks on old photographs, hers wasn't so. She could never dull the image or shut out the memory. Her eyes would be closed but the images would stand right in front of her eyes. She blocked her ears with the thumbs of her hands, yet the sounds she heard continued to deafen her. The sights and sounds worked inside her, running over and over inside her very being as she watched the days go by. Engamma's fears never abated. They lived inside of her, they lived off her, and soon they took over her whole being, looking out at the world through her eyes, showing the world what they had seen and heard, so the world too was afraid to look and hear her fears.

Engamma's husband's stomach was set ablaze for refusing to allow the boys to leave with the men that walked into their home, dressed in tiger stripes. The boys were very small, only five and seven years old.

"They are too young," her husband pleaded, but his words didn't have a sound.

The men in tiger stripes saw his lips move and his arms rise to hold back the boys, and they emptied the contents of a barrel of fire inside his stomach. Taka-taka-taka-taka-taka it sounded, as the barrel spat out fire into the core of his belly. The outer cover splattered in tiny fragments flying in all directions to fall like a design against the wall closest to where he stood. The intestines jumped out and slithered all over the floor like snakes thrown out from the old charmer's basket. Five rivers of red spluttered out like the water from the holes made in the polythene bag the children played with. He fell to the ground and the thick red blood ran in around him on the floor. They poured more fire into his body as the screams shook the walls of the hut and threw up the roof.

Engamma fell to the ground and touched the feet of the boy dressed in tiger stripes. He was standing inside the door holding her sons by their arms as though they were made out of pieces of old cloth knotted together. He laughed in her face and kicked her. She shrank back in shock. She could feel the tiny child inside her jump. Their laughter mocked her as they left the house dragging the boys like rag dolls against the harsh, dry earth. She lay there, next to her husband, adding translucent rivers to the red rivers that flowed from him as he stared unblinking at the spot near the door where the children left.

Engamma lay there the whole night whimpering like a wounded animal. There was blood on her face and clothes, but she didn't seem to notice this. It was her husband's blood. She seemed to have lost sense of space and time. All she could see was the blood flying out of her husband's stomach and smacking the wall, much like the paint thrown from the brush of a painter against the canvas, turning it a deep red. Then the picture changed to show her the two boys' faces, the looks on their faces as they were dragged away from her against their will. All she heard was the sound of the fire barrel as it unloaded itself inside her husband and the screams that followed. She saw and heard all this turn round and round, one after the other as the night wore on.

The neighbors found her lying next to her dead husband the next morning. She was covered in blood and the mud from the floor. They couldn't make out what she was saying but they could guess what had happened by seeing the devastation around her. One of the neighbors took her in. They couldn't leave her like that, all alone in that hut with no one to look after her. They picked up a few of her clothes and some other essentials. She could barely walk the short distance to her neighbors' house and had to be helped along. She didn't seem to be able to comprehend what was happening around her. The shock of losing all she had seemed to have taken over and all she seemed capable of doing was whimper incomprehensibly. Her neighbors were afraid for her, just as they were afraid for the other three women who seemed to be in the same situation. Engamma continued to whimper as the days progressed. She didn't know it but there were many like her that had seen and heard the same as she had that night. The living dead, someone called them. She heard that phrase but wasn't sure what it meant or who it was directed at. She continued to whimper.

Someone knew Engamma's relatives living in one of the villages further away and they were informed about what had happened. A few days later when the roads became safe to travel on someone came to claim Engamma, to take the woman who was whimpering and staring at nothing in particular to live with her relatives. It was the same in that village too. But at least the men in tiger stripes did not venture here. Slowly she stopped whimpering and began to take care of herself. There was nothing else to do. She had to go on, if not for her sake, then for the little child growing inside. Every time she heard a loud noise, her fear rose as her hands moved involuntarily towards her stomach as if to protect the child. There was fear all around. It sat on the furniture in the house, nestled inside the cooking pots and swayed in the breeze outside. Nothing could get rid of it. No amount of washing or sweeping or dusting could push off the gnawing fear that hung over the village like an invisible cloud.

Radhika was born six months later. The fear continued in the village and all around. Then a year later the men in green camouflage moved in to the village. They set up house at the end of the village and walked about the perimeter, watching and waiting. The tiger stripes were kept at bay. One could hear them howling in the distance but they didn't appear to want to venture into the area again. There were too many men in green camouflage, and this seemed to deter their movements. The men in green camouflage told Engamma that she could return to her home in her village if she wanted. There were men in green camouflage there too, and it was safe. But she preferred to stay where she was. It was hard but at least she was with her family. They too had lost many, and their collective grief was pooled. It made things easier. They understood each other's feelings, their situations. It felt good to be able to have someone around. She felt a little happier as she watched Radhika play in the little space outside the house that they called a garden. Things seemed to return to the way she had known it. Radhika started going to school. She progressed. Time moved on surely but slowly.

Then the men in green camouflage moved out. They were needed elsewhere, they said. Everything was in order here and it was time to leave. The villagers looked on hesitantly. They were not as sure, but didn't want to voice the unthinkable. They watched in silence as the men in green camouflage packed their things and left. Then the unthinkable happened. No sooner had the men in green camouflage moved out than the men in tiger stripes strutted in swinging their tails and waving their fire irons. Her sister's daughter was dragged out from school. The neighbor's son was thrown into a jeep they had stolen from somewhere. Thankfully Radhika was saved. She had gone to Colombo to meet an aunt who had returned from abroad. Messages were sent to her to remain there, and not to return.

The next day Engamma and her sister's family moved to a camp. They had no choice. It was better this way. No more tiger stripes to torment them. They didn't take anything except a change of clothes and some pieces of jewelry. It was hard in the camp, living as they did with hardly any water, privacy or the proper facilities of a house. But it was better than the fear surrounding the house and village they lived in.

But it seemed that Engamma had more luggage than most of the others living in the camp. Engamma carried pictures of her two sons in her mind. She had many pictures. She had brought the family album with her. It had travelled many miles but had not seen any wear or tear. It was well cared for inside the expanse of her mind. There was a photograph of the birth of her two sons, their first hesitant steps, their smiles, looks of amazement, joy, sadness. She had preserved them well. She also had the last photograph, of being dragged out of the house. She had them all. She had stopped counting the years. They must both be grown men now and hardly recognizable. Would she know it was them if she saw them on the street? She couldn't be sure. Radhika was living in Colombo. She had stayed on after her aunt had left. It was better this way. Life in the city was no different, it had its moments too, but at least she was getting an education. The aunt from abroad, a distant relative of her father's, had found her a place to stay with a friend. But the fear still remained. It would always remain.

Sometime later Engamma returned to her village and her old home. There was nowhere else she could go. Her sister preferred to remain in the camp as her village now belonged to the tiger stripes and she didn't want to slave for them.

Engamma was getting old. She wanted to be in the house her husband built. The house where she had her children; The house that held her life. Radhika was safe in the city. She didn't like to think of Radhika living there all alone but the woman who ran the boarding house was kind and took care of the girls like her own. Radhika had found a job and was earning enough to spend on extra classes she took in the evenings. They had decided it would be best for Radhika to remain there. There was no use in returning to the village. It was no place for her. Engamma didn't want to move to the city. It was no place for her. She felt lost and useless. There was nothing for her to do there in the city. No one knew her; no one understood what she was going through, not even Radhika, although she tried. Engamma didn't want to live in that strange place, with its strange sounds and sights. Her place was here in the village in that small house they had called home. She returned with a small bundle of things she had been given at the camp. A change of clothes, some food, a little money and a big album full of photographs stacked neatly inside her mind.

The door creaked open as Engamma rested her hand lightly on the door knob. She dropped her bundle to the floor inside the door and stepped inside. There was nothing left in the house except a few pieces of furniture, millions of particles of dust and a thousand and one memories.

Engamma stood there and stared for a long time at the spot where she had last seen her husband. She could see him lying there with his back to the wall staring at the doorway a look of pain on his face. The faint traces of blood that had splashed against the wall and floor were still visible to her. The boys' little frightened faces stared at her. She could see them silhouetted against the doorway. She could hear their sobbing and the sneering laughter of the men in tiger stripes as they pulled the children away from her. Engamma tried to say something but the words stuck inside her throat and refused to move out. They beat against her chest trying to find a way out but there was nothing she could do. She stared at the scene for a long time as the tears flowing from her eyes and dropping to the parched floor below. Slowly she walked in and squatted on the ground in the middle of the tiny room facing the door and waited for her sons to return.

# The Boy from Wellawatte

Ahmed Rizvi Mohammed returned from London. He had gone there for his BA. Not to meet the Queen, although he would dearly have liked to have a chat with the old girl. He returned home for the summer vacation because his father thought it was better for the boy to be home during the holidays. No knowing what he might be up to with so much time to waste. Better waste it here at home.

"Boys nowadays..." his father said to his wife sprawled in front of the television set. "Who knows what mischief he might get into with those foreign women."

A ticket was bought and sent. Ahmed was on the next plane back home happy to be returning but also a trifle sad he wasn't going to have the fun he had planned to have during his summer break.

Ahmed prided himself on being trilingual like most of his brethren in Sri Lanka. He was very fluent in Tamil, his mother tongue; could manage to make himself understood in Sinhala, the language he spoke to his friends and those at the place he worked at prior to his study; and he could converse in broken English, the language he studied in school and spoke to with his uncle living next door to him in Wellawatte. His uncle was trying to get him a job as a management trainee at the pharmaceutical company after he graduated.

"If he goes to Britain, he will have a degree in Business Administration from a British University," Ahmed's father had told his brother.

Ahmed's father wanted him to study business administration. It was the way to go. He had no intention of seeing his son turn into some arty farty fellow. It would be good for the family to have someone with a British degree. It might even turn the boy around. He was beginning to dream of a new life for the boy who had done nothing in the past to warrant anything but a thumping good smack on his rear end. The boy seemed to spend too much time hanging around with theatre people. It wasn't good. He needed to grow up and start behaving like a man. Acting was not for the likes of him. No one in the family had been in the theatre. It was just not done. Besides, how would he earn a living by acting? No, it wasn't to be, Ahmed's father thought as he stared at the boy reading a comic book. He spoke in earnest to his brother, and his brother agreed. Ahmed's uncle knew the second cousin of the man whose nephew's sister-in-law worked at this company, and though the link was rather vague and long, it was something worth trying. His motto was that every string that could be pulled should be pulled as one of them might pull in some good luck. So he pulled every conceivable string he could get his hands on. And when he couldn't find any strings worth pulling he would create ones for the pulling. The manager of the branch was consulted. The link was secured. The manager agreed to consider taking Ahmed in if he got himself qualified. The manager hadn't given anything in writing, but it was implicitly understood that all that was required was a piece of paper that said Degree in Business Administration with the name and logo of the foreign university. Everything seemed settled.

Hareem Mohammed was the elder brother of Ahmed's father. He did business; all kinds of business. But his knack it seemed was in the string business. He was the best string puller this side of Wellawatte, and all his relatives and friends had benefited from his influences at some time or the other. Whenever there was a need for anything, a job, reference to a school, finding a doctor or even buying a ticket to go abroad, Hareem was consulted. It was better and more profitable than consulting the stars, all his beneficiaries claimed. They had checked their respective stars but had found them wanting in some department or the other. Maybe the stars were losing their influence after so many centuries of being consulted. Maybe the astrologers had pushed one too many buttons of the stars and they had decided not to tell. Or maybe the stars were just tired of hanging around all dressed up every night with no place to go except the same old spot on the sky and nothing much to do but grin and shine like the fancy painted women hovering around the night spots of the city. Maybe, like everyone else, the stars too were now charging and needed a little extra something to get their creative juices running. Maybe the encouragement the people were offering wasn't enough. Of course the Hindus were praying to them every day as always, and the Buddhists were making offerings to this and that temple or Kovil. But the Muslims and Christians didn't seem to be making an effort and this may have been the problem. There were many Muslims and Christians who visited the astrologers, although they weren't really supposed to mingle with the likes of astrologers, but in a day and age when people needed all the help they could to survive, what was wrong with asking a favor or two from the stars. After all, they surmised, politicians were being consulted and their favors sought, then why not the stars?

But then came Hareem like a savior to them all. The astrologers grumbled as they vied for the purses of the desperate with Hareem.

"That fellow is putting us out of a job," one astrologer complained to his astrologer-friend.

They had met at the market and were checking out brinjals before buying.

A.M. Porolis was the senior of the two. He came from a long line of astrologers and was considered something of an expert for his years of training and inherent family knowledge. A.M. Porolis had been living in Wellawatte for most of his life. His family had moved to Colombo, when his father, old man that he was, became the main man for the Prime Minister. The family decided to stay back after his father passed away although the Prime Minister lost the next election because the astrologer they hurriedly consulted wasn't in tune with the stars like old man Porolis had been.

Ranaweera Mudianse, the other astrologer, was from Galle. His family lineage wasn't as impressive as Porolis's but it was impressive enough. He had moved to Wellawatte in the nineteen eighties as many of his clients were from Colombo and the surrounding areas and he wanted to be close by, especially since most of them didn't always have the time to make it all the way to Galle. Business was very good, that is until the fame of Hareem spread, shrouding the roads to the two astrologers' houses like an old woman's black burqua.

"What is a Muslim doing in this business?" Porolis asked "I thought their religion didn't allow them to cast horoscopes?"

"What has religion to do with anything nowadays?" Ranaweera Mudianse grumbled. "It is only used for personal gains and not for the reasons of belief and harmony."

"Someone should complain to the Maulavi about this unreligious act" Porolis said.

"I bet the Maulavi knows about it and is keeping quiet," spat out Ranaweera Mudianse in disgust. "I heard he is getting a cut. One of my clients told me the Maulavi down the road has got his horoscope cast to find out if it would be a good time for him to enter politics."

Porolis grunted in disgust.

"My clients are now asking me to pull strings for them in addition to reading their horoscopes. What is the world coming to?" He pointed at two brinjals with his walking stick. "Give me those two," he said to the vegetable man.

"Well, I'll be on my way," Ranaweera Mudianse said picking up his change from the vegetable man. The two men parted company.

Hareem knew a little about horoscopes as well. He wasn't as proficient at reading them as were the real astrologers but he could manage to figure out, as any normal person could, the significance of the planets positions in each house on the life of the particular person. This was enough. This and his craftsmanship at string pulling. Hareem wasn't too fond of his brother's son. He was a real scoundrel if ever there was one. He would have liked to thrash the fellow blue and black with the broom, but it would not have been of much use except to injure the broom. And then he would have to get his wife another one. But he was after all family and Hareem grudgingly agreed to do his bit for the boy. Phone calls were made. People were spoken to and shoulders were patted. Someone agreed to tutor Ahmed in English. Mr. Lester de Silva, the tutor in question wasn't very proficient in the language. He knew his grammar inside out, but his pronunciation was as atrocious as a cat trying to speak like a parrot. But it didn't matter. All that was needed was to get Ahmed up to something a little above a "Hi – Bye" standard. Enough to convince the visa officer at the British High Commission in Colombo and the Immigration Officer at Heathrow that he was able to get along with life in Britain. So they worked on him, day and night, night and day until they were all exhausted.

Ahmed scraped through the English Language Proficiency test. A very big string was released and then pulled in to secure a place at a University in Britain and everything was all set. It was somewhere in Essex or Sussex, the uncle couldn't remember where. Ahmed didn't care. As long as he was going to Britain was all that he cared. He had not been very keen on going but after hearing about the good time everyone seemed to be having there, Ahmed had turned around. He had started making plans and dreaming big dreams of his new life in Britain, that didn't necessarily involve getting himself a degree. He really didn't care where in Britain he was going as long as he got there, was what he wanted to say to his uncle who had looked him up and down, but his uncle had looked so stern that Ahmed decided to keep shut.

Ahmed got himself to Britain but once there it was hard work. It wasn't what he had quite expected. His English, though quite okay by foreign students' standards wasn't enough to convince the professors at the University.

"You need extra coaching in English," one of them said after reading a paper on Keats submitted by Ahmed who had decided he wanted to study English Literature and not Business Administration, much to his father's annoyance.

He had been sent to study Business Administration but it seemed that in the process of completing the application form Ahmed had mistakenly ticked the column that said English Literature. The word mistakenly to be read within inverted commas. His father had no idea about his son's little game plan and only heard about it much later when it was too late. So there was Ahmed studying English Literature and thrilled to bits. The paper he had written seemed to be about Keats but it was written in words so strange that it was like reading a horror story. It was no wonder the poor professor had been aghast and had turned a bright florescent pink. Here was the cream of British poetry being churned around in mud by this upstart from an ex-colony. What was the world coming to? He held his head in his hands and sighed into his chest.

Ahmed started taking English classes. It was hard. He hated it but he didn't have a choice. Although he had been tutored to "Hi-Bye" standards, his was really something of a "not–pot" syndrome. But then most of the other students were no better. The East Europeans that were flooding into Britain like the Danube gone astray spoke an English that even they couldn't understand amongst themselves. It was far worse than the "not-pot" he spoke. Ahmed was stunned. He went into culture shock. He seemed to be the most fluent amongst all of them. He was elated.

"I speak better English than all of these people here," he proudly wrote back to his father.

The father in turn showed the letter around to all and sundry.

"Look, look my son speaks better English than the people in Britain. If he stays longer he might even speak better than the Queen!"

Hareem read the letter and was awestruck. Maybe the boy wasn't so bad after all, he pondered scratching the bald spot on his round head. There was still room for hope.

The English tutor was elated. One of his students had not only got himself into a posh English University, but he was speaking better English than the British and it was all his hard work. Parents with hopes of English dreams for their offspring flocked to Lester de Silva's residence with their children.

"Teach my son to speak like that Rizvi boy and get him to England," they requested the tutor.

Lester de Silva nodded his head and promised them an English -speaking son in a year. The parents were overjoyed. The English tutor increased his fees.

Meanwhile Ahmed's status at home had increased tenfold. He was the talk of the relatives. He refused to speak anything other than English to his family after he returned for the holidays. They were amused, but indulged him.

"He needs to practice his English," Ahmed's mother said proudly to the neighbor.

"Thambi!" his friend Yoosuf yelled out on the street when he and a group of friends saw Ahmed approaching.

They stood at the side of the road and beckoned to Ahmed to come over. Ahmed smiled to see his friends. He crossed the road and joined the group as they began an animated conversation in Tamil.

"What's it like in Britain? Did you meet Nazir? Did you visit the Queen girl?"

They all began talking at the same time. They had been hanging around the Bombay Sweets Shop sipping on faludas when they saw Ahmed walk by. They were happy to see their friend and Ahmed was in turn happy to see his old school friends. But a pained look crossed Ahmed's face the moment his friends started to speak.

"What's the matter, Ahmed brother?" Murugan asked on seeing the look on his face.

The others stopped their joking and looked with concern.

"Yes, what's up? Are you in pain?" they asked, concerned that their friend might have caught some unknown British disease.

They questioned him in Tamil and Sinhala, the languages they all spoke. Ahmed looked more and more pained as the words flew around him.

"Ah, ah, ah..." he mumbled as they spoke to him, to each other.

"What's the matter? Tell brother, tell?" Even the cashier looked out of the shop with concern.

"Bring the boy inside. Maybe the sun is too hot for him. Someone get him some water," he called out with concern.

The boys trouped in behind Ahmed. A glass of water was offered to him.

"What happened in Britain, Ahmed brother? Did they torture you? Did they think you were Al-Qaeda? These foreigners, they think all Muslims are terrorists. What did they do to you?" someone asked.

"No," Ahmed finally replied faintly in English. "Nothing like that."

"Then what's the matter?" Asif asked.

"I find it difficult to explain," Ahmed said taking another sip of water.

"Try brother, try. We have all the time in the world and no place to go," Yoosuf said.

"I'm not sick," Ahmed said slowly.

"That's good to know," Riaz said. "But why are you speaking in English? Have you forgotten how to speak in Tamil?'

Ahmed looked up at Riaz and nodded.

"Yes brother, I find it hard to speak in Tamil. It's been so long. I have not spoken a single word for the past six months."

Yoosuf's mouth flew open at the comment. He was sitting right next to Ahmed sipping on his faluda. The straw did a double take and popped out of his mouth and out of the glass onto the floor. The faluda that had moved up the straw towards Yoosuf's mouth fell on to his shirt-front in dismay at not being able to make it to his mouth. Yoosuf didn't notice it. Riaz too was lost for words. The others just gaped. Then Riaz managed to find words.

"But how can anyone forget the language they spoke all their life?" he asked, sounding perplexed.

"That's what I also can't understand," Ahmed said in English, a strange non-English accent accompanying the words. "But it happened."

"What about Sinhala, can you at least speak that?" Murugan asked.

"What? Oh. Sinhala. No, I have forgotten that as well," Ahmed said.

"Try brother, try. Say something in Sinhala." Riaz insisted.

Ahmed stared into his glass of water. He didn't know how to respond. They didn't seem convinced and Ahmed left it at that. Besides what could he say?

"Listen you all," he added finally, his heavily accentuated English accent getting more accentuated all the time, "I really need to be going. I have some errands to run. Good bye boys. Let's meet for drinks later on, shall we?"

Ahmed stepped out of the shop before anyone could answer. He really didn't feel like talking to them or trying to explain. They wouldn't understand. They were like a herd of village buffalos that had got lost in town. They didn't even speak properly, but shouted at each other and made crude remarks that were not in keeping with the changing trends of the day. They were extremely backward and Ahmed felt a tad ashamed to be seen with them. He vowed to make every effort to avoid them if he could. He had risen up in the world, he was after all studying in Britain; something none of them could have even dreamed of. They were such losers, he sniffed with disdain. He, Ahmed Rizvi Mohammed was better than any of them, he was going places and needed to maintain his new social status that had no place for the likes of them. Ahmed scowled as the small boy standing aimlessly at the side of the road grinned at him. His friends were like that; aimless and directionless with silly grins on their faces. He lifted his head high and hurried away.

The others stared at his departing figure.

"What happened to the brother?" Riaz asked perplexed. "Is it really possible to forget a language like that?"

"I don't know. Maybe it is," Murugan said.

"How long has he been away?" Yoosuf asked.

"Six months, I think."

"Six months! Only six months! No impossible. I think he is just pretending."

"He is such a fake."

"He has caught a disease after all – the 'can't remember his own language' disease," Riaz said.

Howls of laughter followed this comment. Even the cashier was amused.

"What a thing to happen. This too, to a boy who couldn't speak English in the first place. Now he knows too much English that he has forgotten how to speak the other languages." He hooted for his workers to hear.

# Breaking News

Pauline cried when Rohana Wijeweera died. She saw a picture of him in the papers and this was what made her cry. Not the mention of his death but the sight of the picture in the papers. It may be surmised that the picture reinforced the news she had heard both officially through the media and unofficially through the local grapevine, that the man was dead. Chris was with her when it happened, although neither of them knew it at that time. They were relaxing with a beer at Otters, talking about the exhibition they had just seen.

The man had died when the army stormed his secret hideout and pulled him out by the scuff of his neck. They said he howled like a jackal and begged them to spare his life. The army wasn't interested in the crocodile tears and had shot him dead, or so it was said. The real gruesome manner in which he died would be revealed much, much later. But for the moment that seemed to be the version that took wing. He had died on the spot. Just like that. In ice cold blood, although that is merely an expression of speech and the temperature of the blood cannot be gauged by a mere expression of speech. For all you know it could have been warm or even hot but the expression of speech turned it cold as it desired best. Maybe his blood ran cold all over the floor and over the walls and tried to make it out of the window for some fresh air, or maybe it started off red hot and then ran cold as it splashed out of the man. They say he died before he could negotiate a deal for him to move to Russia, his preferred place in the world, and never return - along with his colleagues, although no mention was made about their begging. But it is safe to conclude that they too followed their leader's example and burst into manly tears at the thought of having to end their lives right then and there.

Everyone at home was stunned when Pauline cried. They had been talking about it the previous evening when she had returned late and could not figure out why it had taken so long for her to grasp the news. It wasn't like her to miss out on anything. She was usually the first to comment on anything that happened. So what had gone wrong? Was she getting senile they wondered, rather worried at the thought of a senile and forgetful Pauline on their hands. Was she perhaps taking after grandaunt Clotilda who had gone off her head a year after her marriage? It was rumored that the family inheritance, as they called it, was passed down the centuries. Why even their mother Gertrude had begun showing signs of the madness. Had it chosen to make an appearance in Pauline? Rupert her brother, the eldest in the family and their sister Sujatha exchanged worried looks.

They had been anticipating something like this to happen and had been wondering who would be the chosen one in their generation to carry on the family inheritance. Now it seemed at least they were saved. Pauline seemed to be the chosen one. But she was still young, not yet past her forties. Yet one could never be certain. Could it be possible? Here she was crying real big tears at the news of the man's death.

They had no idea she was such a huge fan of the Marxist troublemaker who had brought their lives to a standstill those few years with his madness against the establishment. Pauline was from a high class family living in the posh suburbs of Colombo. Getting involved in anything remotely Marxist or revolutionary was the last thing one would have expected of Pauline. Her life was in stark contrast to the life and ideology espoused by Rohana Wijeweera and his gang of local hoodlums. She partied till the wee hours of the morning with whichever man she was seeing at the moment. She dressed in Western clothes made in the West – mostly in America, that pothole of corruption and materialism. Drank herself silly and travelled to all the important capitals of the world for want of anything better to do.

Pauline had a lot of admirers, all equally well-bred English educated people like herself. She had studied at a private school in Colombo and was whiling her time writing to the newspapers: The English press. She had no idea how to string a sentence in Sinhala and rolled her eyes up to the heavens if anyone mentioned Tamil. She was an exclusive member of the unwritten social minority that lived in Sri Lanka but professed an ideology that was as distant as the shores of the North Pole.

It wasn't that Pauline or the Crowd, as they referred to themselves, was unpatriotic. They were the most devoutly patriotic people any country could ever ask for. When the Indo-Lanka pact was forced on the country by India, they were the first to protest the injustice of the Indian government in meddling in the affairs of the country. When the Indian air force violated all norms of International Law, entering Sri Lankan airspace and dropping food for the so-called starving people in the north, they were ready to get on the streets and march to the Indian High Commissioner's house to protest. It did not matter that half the Crowd spent their time hobnobbing with the diplomats stationed in Colombo and spending time at the various embassy parties and get-togethers. What was wrong was wrong, and they believed something had to be done. They were prevented in their march by the non appearance of Sudhu, the self- proclaimed artist who had quarreled with his lover and had thus forgotten to prepare the banners for the march. The people waited and waited and finally Nimal went searching for Sudhu, only to find him sprawled on the living room sofa at his house in a pool of tears. Nimal spent the better half of the morning consoling the man, and only then did he hear about the lack of banners. The march was called off. Pauline and her friends retired to the Galle Face Hotel for lunch and to talk about the new development with Sudhu.

Sudhu was an artist by profession. He lived in a small flat in Kollupitiya overlooking the sea. When he was not painting, he was organizing fashion shows and sometimes even modeling, although he couldn't really be called a model as he was too scraggy. But most of the time he painted, travelling to remote corners of the country in search of inspiration. Nayantara, Pauline's school friend, was Sudhu's sponsor for his various exhibitions. She had a strange affinity for the boy and was quite taken up by his paintings although no one else in the Crowd shared her views. They were rather boring and drab subjects and Sudhu didn't really have much talent, but no one had the heart to tell this to him. He was a good soul and they were all quite fond of him. If he wanted to paint strange paintings, who were they to complain. It was only Nayantara that seemed to understand his paintings and promoted him as the next best thing to sliced bread although it had to be said that there were many other things that were of greater value that had followed the invention of sliced bread. Still it was Nayantara's time and money, and if she wanted to spend her family's money on buying space at the Lionel Wendt for

Sudhu's exhibitions and hosting parties for him, then who were they to object. Besides, most of them were invited to the pre-exhibition parties and they were happy for Sudhu although Nayantara's cousin Manel often complained, but no one listened to her anyway.

So why did Pauline cry? Rupert, Sujatha and their mother Gertrude dropped their work and rushed out to the verandah to see what the fuss was about. They thought Pauline had fallen down and hurt herself. They saw her holding the newspaper, and then they thought she had read about an accident to one of her past admirers.

"Here let me see that."

Rupert snatched the paper from her hand and glanced through the news items. He could find none about anyone they knew. He quickly ran his eye over the obituaries but there was nothing there too. His brow creased into a puzzle as he looked up at Pauline. Gertrude, standing with her hand on the door frame for balance, rasped out something no one understood. She was getting on in years and it was getting harder and harder to make out anything she said, or even did. They all tried to be patient with her but the collective pot of patience they had been doling out was fast emptying and no one wanted to be the first to mention what would happen when it did all run out. Sujatha took Pauline's hand and directed her towards a chair at the edge of the verandah. Pauline was sniffing into her hanky and crying genuine salty tears that ran down her cheeks and down her neck to get lost in the collar of her blouse.

"What's all this?" Sujatha asked gently.

"He's dead," she whimpered sinking into the chair.

"Who is?" Sujatha asked patting her arm.

"That guy. Rohana Wijeweera is dead," Pauline sniffed.

Sujatha and Rupert exchanged looks. They had no idea that Pauline knew Rohana Wijeweera. Could she have by some chance met him on campus when she was studying? Did they have an affair that none of them knew about? Why, he must be at least two decades older than she? What could they possibly have in common? The family was very open about whom they dated, and although Gertrude sometimes frowned on the arty-farty lot that wafted through the doors, she too didn't give much opposition to any of the men that passed through the lives of her two daughters.

"I didn't know that you were friends with him?" Sujatha said gently.

"Who, that man? Are you crazy!" Pauline stopped her sniffing to stare stupefied at her elder sister. "What in the world possessed you to think I knew him?" she said and sat up in her chair.

"Well," Sujatha hesitated. "We thought you may have met him on campus or something like that."

Pauline stared at her brother and sister as if they had gone off their heads, then she threw back her mane of black curly hair and sent off a hoot of laughter that shocked Fluffy, the ugly old Pomeranian bitch. Fluffy gave one startled yelp and ran into the house.

"You silly people," she guffawed. "What would I possibly have in common with that man?"

"We were wondering the same thing," Gertrude said in her normal voice that she seemed to reserve for special moments. "To think you might be a Marxist. You almost sent me to my grave early. What would your poor father have thought?" she spluttered.

"What! Me a Marxist? You are all mad," Pauline exclaimed, stunned that anyone could even remotely consider her as one of those people.

It turned out that Pauline was crying because the picture in the papers showed a different person from the one everyone was accustomed to seeing. Rohana Wijeweera in the posters had a dirty ragged beard that ran along his jaw from one ear to the other, left to right like a curve along his face. He wore his hair curly and long which he covered with a cap and wore thick black-framed spectacles. That was the image of the man that was used in posters and in the newspapers when they published any story about him. But this picture of him, a man who looked frail and weak, pale skinned and shaven with well-combed hair was nothing like the person he was supposed to be.

"You mean to say you are crying because he looks different?" Rupert exclaimed in stupefied astonishment.

He could never understand women, and living for forty something years with his sisters and mother had not made it any easier. Every day brought him something new when he thought he had seen it all. He scratched his brow and stared at Pauline.

"He looks so pathetic," she wailed. "Nothing like the pictures in the posters," she declared. "I'm sure they got the wrong man."

"The army can't have made a mistake like that," Sujatha said.

"But what if they did?" Pauline asked staring up at her brother. "Aiyah, don't you have a friend who is in the army? Why don't you call him up and ask him if they made a mistake."

She rose from her chair and moved towards her brother.

"Yes Aiyah, why don't you do that?" Sujatha added.

She too was beginning to get caught up on the moment and it did look as though Pauline might have hit on something. What if they got the wrong man? That was a serious situation. She looked expectantly at her brother.

"You are both mad as hatters!" Rupert exclaimed, adding firmly, "I will not call anyone and ask them something so ridiculous."

"But he doesn't look like Rohana Wijeweera?" she wailed.

"You're right, he doesn't."

Sujatha scrutinized the picture from all angles like a makeup artist trying to find the best of the person's features. She had seen Shah Jahan, their hairdresser cum makeup artist scrutinizing pictures of brides-to-be for the best way to do their makeup. He had, seeing her interest, given her a few tips on how to study a face before deciding on how to make up the face.

"Here, let me see that."

Gertrude spluttered like a frying pan and held her frail arm towards her daughters. The paper was passed to her. She peered at the picture for a full three minutes before giving it back.

"I would have thought it was something wrong with my eyesight, but it is not him. They got the wrong man. Rupert, what do you think?" she demanded and thrust the paper in his face.

"Maybe it's because he has shaved in the picture," Rupert sighed.

"It's not that the facial hair is missing or the hair cut is different, even his skin is fairer, much fairer," Sujatha exclaimed.

"Maybe he got some skin disease like Michael Jackson."

They stared at each other in amazement like only sisters can.

"Maybe he got white spots like kabara that spread all over his face."

The girls giggled at the image of a kabara Rohana Wijeweera.

"And maybe he applied makeup and wore a wig and pasted a beard for the other photographs, or when he met the people," Sujatha gasped out.

"Or maybe it's because he spent so much time in hiding. Maybe the underground air in the bunkers turned his skin white," Pauline said.

"Yes, that may be it. Maybe the lack of sunshine all those years turned him several shades lighter. And maybe he got kabara after that," Sujatha added.

"Or maybe he got kabara, that's why he hid in a bunker," Pauline reasoned.

"Boy, he must have felt like a real Kabaragoya!" Sujatha exclaimed.

Gertrude let out a hoot of laughter. The girls looked at their mother and giggled like schoolchildren.

"This means even Prabakaran may look different!"

Pauline's remarks brought a sobering silence to the group. Even Fluffy who had returned to the verandah lowered her head to a side in contemplation.

"Do you think he too has turned into a Kabaragoya?" Sujatha asked.

"We will have to wait and see what he looks like," Pauline added. "Oh I hope the army gets him soon. We could compare the pictures."

"What fun. And maybe you can write an article on the similarities of the two thugs and how they controlled their image," Sujatha said.

Pauline shrieked in delight at her sister's comments.

"You are a genius!" she exclaimed putting her arm round her and planting a huge kiss on her cheek. "Let's go call the others and tell them."

# Like Driftwood on the Kelani

Sweeneetha stood still on the Kelani bridge as the twilight played with her hair. She pushed back a wisp of hair that fell across her cheek and gazed down at the swirling muddy waters of the Kelani river as it moved silently to the sea. Sweeneetha watched the waters ripple black grey as it moved furiously under the bridge, taking with it whatever floated in its way. The rains had swollen the Kelani and it moved like a drunken bus driver sullenly, brooding, wanting nothing more than to stop in its tracks to rest awhile. She couldn't stand here for too long lest she attract the attention of the security personnel standing guard at the entrance of the bridge towards the city of Colombo. She looked towards the place where they were standing and sighed. The traffic screeched past behind her on the road unaware of her intentions or purpose on the bridge; the waters swirled silently below willing her to come closer and take a look. She turned and walked slowly towards the pathway that led to the houses at the side of the river.

No one was allowed to pause on the Kelani bridge for any reason. It was a security zone, now manned by army personnel who patrolled the area and checked on vehicles entering the city. The security checks were because of the terrorist threats. Someone might try to strap a bomb to the railings and blow the bridge apart. This was the greatest fear. It wouldn't cause many deaths like a bomb in a vehicle during rush hour traffic, but the inconvenience to the public would be immense. It had always been looked on a little askew when anyone stopped on the bridge. People had better things to do besides stand on a bridge and watch the waters swirl by. It was only those who were jobless and aimless that had the time for such luxuries. Most others were not so fortunate.

There was a time when dare-devil teenagers living in the shanty on the banks of the river would wager a few bucks to make a clean dive off the bridge. However those days were long past. Anyone making the plunge now would not be doing so for such pleasurable reasons. If anything, it was to wager with the devil himself that they would succeed and end their lives right there in the river. It was said that for those people who made the wager before letting themselves fly off the bridge, the devil did listen and guide their descent to the deepest point in the river so that if anyone were to dive in after them in an attempt to rescue, the rescuers wouldn't succeed, as the plunge would take the person plunging in way too down under. But now even that was not so easy to attempt with the security personnel patrolling the bridge.

The public really didn't care about the suicides. It was one less miserable life to contend with. Besides who were they, and what right did they have to interfere in someone else's destiny? If someone wanted out he could have out. Life these days wasn't worth living. Who were they to complain if someone wanted to end his or her life right there in the river? What was one death in comparison to all those forced deaths of the disappeared?

The Kelani was a reluctant participant in many a gruesome deed. Some said she witnessed the mangled scarred bodies of the young every night as they were brought into her. She bore them gently to the sea but the sight of so many so frequently had angered her. It was a revolt against nature and the Kelani protested in the only way she knew how. She willed the rains to fill her up so she could throw up the bodies to the banks to let the others know what she was forced to do. The people living on the banks were horrified by what they saw, but after a while they too became silent spectators. Protesting about the bodies appearing in the water got them into trouble. If a bloated body appeared close to their homes, they merely gave it a shove towards the current. They had become accustomed to being surprised by the sudden appearance of a body popping up next to them as if to get one last breath inside the already water-logged body, or one last look at the night sky before the body was belched into the sea, to be thrown against the rocks and boulders by the crashing waves as it devoured the flesh slowly, slowly in a gruesome dance until there was nothing that remained. Nothing to show who it had been, where it had come from, or where it was going. The sea was thorough in its work and the Kelani knew it. Maybe that was why she tried to provide some comfort, a respite before the next attack.

The river people had stopped counting the bodies a long time ago. It was of absolutely no use anymore. It was just a waste of time as they couldn't possibly keep track of so many. It wasn't their job anyway. The police should do it. But the police neither came to collect the bodies or count them as they floated by. It was as if the police had other things on their mind and the death of the young was of no consequence to them. The old man living at the furthest end of the river had started keeping a record of sorts, but the human floats had grown so numerous that he too soon gave up after a few weeks. He was too old and too tired to continue. He was appalled by what he saw and even more so by the lack of interest shown by the police. He tried to protest but the other people stopped him with pleas. They sensed there was a reason for all this and didn't want to get involved in someone else's game. They stayed in their small homes and watched in silence as the bodies moved like pieces of driftwood on the Kelani as it glided swiftly towards the ocean not so far away. No one knew where the bodies joined the Kelani. Some said it was far away, some said it was from the town on the other side. But no one knew for sure. No one that is, except for those who fed the Kelani with the bodies like it was some large crocodile, and the Kelani itself.

Fear set in slowly. The game of watching the bodies float was no longer a game. Not the kind they knew of anyway. The rules were far too complex for their simple minds. This was a deadly serious game and they neither knew the rules nor the players. It was a game nevertheless, a fight to the death, played with an invisible dice thrown by an invisible hand. A pawn was found and the game was played and the loser ended in the river, scarred, bruised and sometimes barely alive. What the game began the river was forced to complete whether she liked it or not.

So they stayed inside and hardly spoke about it even with their immediate neighbors. It was as if they'd silently imposed a censor on all their words, thoughts and actions. Death was a word that was taboo from that day on.

The river people hardly spent much time in the river now. It had been their source of enjoyment. They had sported in the river, the children had spent hours playing in the water, the women bathed leisurely, all the while taking in the silent gentle swirl of the waters as it moved on its way guided by the calls of the water birds sitting on the breezes overhead. But now it was different and they were forced to change their way of life. They no longer spent time in the river for enjoyment. It was only for necessity now. The river people had become accustomed to bumping into a bloated dead, but the fear that arose at the sight was beginning to have an effect. They began controlling their movements in the river to avoid seeing anything they shouldn't see. It was better that way. Besides it wasn't safe to be out during the curfew even for a night's dip at the back of one's own house.

But last night it had been different. The bodies started floating before the curfew hour when people were still going about their daily chores. Twilight was deepening and the last chores were being performed: washing, cleaning and collecting water for the night. It caused quite a stir and everyone suddenly broke their silence and began to talk in excited whispers.

Namal's uncle was in the river when the bodies floated by. The next morning, just as the curfew broke, Namal made his way to Sweeneetha's house to tell her. He would meet her at the office on Monday, but by then it might be too late. She needed to know now. However gruesome it might be she needed to know. She had a right to know.

This was what had brought Sweeneetha to the river that evening. Namal's uncle hadn't been able to recognize any of the bodies, bloated and disfigured as they were. And he couldn't be of much help. They had taken her to where the bodies had piled up at the side on the bank, but no one was willing to move them lest the water soaked flesh came out like wet sticky mud into their hands.

"For all you know they may be people from some remote village. It happens, you know."

Namal's uncle told her, attempting to comfort her as he and Namal stood with her at the river's edge. He knew it was a feeble attempt made by someone who could not reach the depths of despair but only touch the surface.

But Sweeneetha knew that this time it wasn't a false alarm. She could feel it and sense it. She stood there looking at the rotting smelling pile of flesh piled one on top of the other, disfigured and in disarray. No one wanted to get close to the heap, not even the flies that seemed to be in shock and tried to keep their distance. She had nothing to say, no words to utter to that pile lying there. She stood there for an eternity. Her life story flashed before her projecting itself onto the pile of rotting slimy carcasses. She stood there seemingly unaware of the stench, unable to move, to speak. She sighed and blinked her eyes as the story flashed to its end. Then she turned around and moved back, retracing her steps. Namal and his uncle followed silently behind her. They didn't know what to say or do. How did you console a person that has gone through it all and has come to the very end, the precipice that looks down at what might have been? They had seen many bodies but had not witnessed the depth of emotion felt by someone who had come hoping to claim something, anything, but had to leave with nothing. No answers to the questions that were bursting to break through, like the waves of the water that pushed everything that stood in its way. They could sense she wanted to know more but was unable to ask them because she too knew that they didn't have the answers she sought.

The people in the houses stopped their work to watch her as she left, a stooped figure carrying a heavy burden of grief, so much heavier than the pots and pans they carried down to the river. They watched her walk away past their meager homes, a world within a world. Sweeneetha took a deep breath and turned towards the two men walking silently behind her. Her smile was a feeble attempt to show them she was ok. They looked down as she thanked them for their help. Then she stepped onto the road and proceeded slowly to the bridge. The sun glowed like bright orange bougainvillea behind a thick cloud. The breezes wafting over the bridge were warm and gentle. There was an answer to her quest at the bottom of that pile of bodies at the side of the river, of that she was certain. But try as she might she could not get herself to ask the men to look through them. That wouldn't have been fair on them. It was not their problem. She couldn't burden them with anything like that. They had already done what they could. She sighed and placed a hand on the railing of the bridge to steady herself. As she gazed down at the hungry waters now heavy with the bodies of the young it had picked up, she knew with a certainty that could only be known by those who lose a loved one that one of those bloated bodies, one of them belonged to him. She knew it in her heart. She was as certain as she had been when she heard that he'd been taken away, that she wouldn't see him again, either alive or dead. And now it was all over. Or was it?

There was no going back. All those months of searching had finally ended. What was she to do now? All her days since the moment he'd been taken away had been consumed with looking for him, searching for him in every place she could think of. Every time someone mentioned a word, uttered a phrase she would gaze hopefully and begin a new search. But now there would be no more journeys. With one surge of the waters it was all over. Such finality. How cold it felt. Had she hardened so much in those few months that she couldn't feel any emotion? No tears? No pain?

Her eyes stung with the unshed tears of the months past. The breeze played with her hair, trying to get her to respond, but it only dried her eyes even more. Her eyes stung with the helplessness of it all, the inability to do anything. The utter waste of time and life. Of unnecessary death. But what could she do? She was as helpless as the rest of them. She stood there, a small figure in the noisy bustle of vehicles passing by behind her. People were making their way back home. No one had the time to notice a girl standing at the bridge. Everyone was in too much of a hurry to get home before the curfew. There was a sense of urgency, of hurry, of wanting to get there. Anywhere, but be on the streets. Down below the Kelani flowed silently, peacefully, or so it seemed. Nothing stopped in its way.

# Sepalika

There was a strange quietness all around. The birds had stopped singing and seemed to have disappeared into the forest. Those that remained were silent. Listening. Waiting for something to happen. For someone to give the call and then they too would move. My father stood outside our little hut and surveyed the vastness of the jungle beyond. The early morning chill surrounded us. I rubbed the sleep from my eyes as I walked towards the back of the house where my mother was preparing the breakfast. It was not yet light and she cooked in the light of the kerosene stove. She saw me standing at the door.

"Go wash your face and get ready for school," she said, ruffling my already tousled hair.

I watched Samanmali, my eldest sister, scraping the coconut for our roti. She was two years older than me but seemed much older. Our younger sister, Sepalika was named after the little white flowers with orange stems that bloom in the early morning. We had a tree at the front of the house and every morning we woke up to the sweet smell of the flowers drifting in the air. The flowers fell to the ground creating a lovely white carpet all around the tree. Sepalika was born in the early morning, when the flowers she was named after, bloomed and perfumed the air. My mother said the little girl reminded her of the flowers in our garden. Everyone was happy with the name. Sepalika was asleep in her tiny cot inside our room.

I walked towards the tree and picked the best flowers that had fallen; some I placed in a tray, sprinkled water on them and offered to the Buddha whose image was inside our house. The rest I put into a bag to take to school to offer to the Buddha image in class. Sometimes Samanmali also took flowers. But it was always I who picked the flowers.

The flowers didn't last long; they wilted in the morning sun and faded by afternoon. That was the way of those flowers. Then again a new lot bloomed in the dawn to perfume all around. There were more flowers today and I filled two bags with flowers and placed them on the low bench at the entrance to our house. Taking an ekel broom I swept the dried leaves that had fallen in the tiny garden during the night. Charulatha, our immediate neighbor was furiously sweeping her side of the garden. She was in a class senior to me. We all travelled to school together: my sister, myself, Charulatha and a few others living in this area. The school was far from our house, in the middle of the next village, and it was a long walk, but I didn't mind as I liked going to school. I liked learning new things, many different and interesting things. I started school three years ago. Not that long ago.

My name is Sagara. I was named after the great ocean that is supposed to encircle the country. I had never seen the ocean but one day I hoped I would. Until then I would live here in my village with my parents and two sisters.

I loved playing with Sepalika just as much as I liked picking the flowers she was named after. She was born four months ago and could barely move, so tiny was she. But she had a lovely smile.

"You will grow up to be just as lovely as the flowers," I told her as I stroked her soft cheek.

She had woken up and was trying to make herself heard. She stared at me with eyes opened wide and cooed in pleasure as I sat by her cot. My mother went to stay with my grandmother in the next town when she was in her third month. Everyone thought it best that she stay away until the baby was born as the stress of living in the village wouldn't have been good for either of them. My aunt came to stay with us during that time. She was my mother's elder sister and could cook better than anyone I knew. When my mother returned two weeks ago, she stayed on to help with the baby.

Samanmali returned shivering after her bath at the well. It was always hard to take a bath in the morning as the water was very cold. It was now my turn to take a bath and get dressed for school. I was about to leave when we heard voices at the front. Appuhamy had stopped by and was talking to my father. They sounded worried. My mother stopped her cooking and listened. My aunt too listened but she was already closing the cooking utensils with lids when my father rushed in and told us we had to leave. They had spotted a gang of men in the area beyond approaching the village. We dropped everything we were doing and rushed out. This had become such a routine that we complied without a moment's pause. We usually took something to eat as there was no knowing how long we would have to be away. But today there was nothing to take. The rotis were ready but the dhal curry was still cooking on the fire. My mother had just placed the last of the rotis on the roti tray on the fire. She forgot to take it off but moved towards the inside and picked up Sepalika.

"What do you think you are doing?" my father asked seeing her carrying Sepalika.

"We can't leave her here alone, can we?" my mother asked looking worried.

"We can't take her either. She might find it difficult in the jungle," my father said.

"What shall we do?" she asked.

"I could stay behind," my aunt offered.

"Don't be silly. They would not show any mercy towards you. But an infant they might not notice," my father said. "She might cry and give us away, if we take her," he added seeing her look of uncertainty.

"That's true. We will be putting everyone in danger," my mother replied slowly. "What shall we do?"

"Cover her up tight and leave her under the bed. They won't find her there. And she won't make a noise if she's inside the house,"my father said after a moment's thought.

My mother stuck a rubber teat in her mouth and quickly covered Sepalika in a pink baby blanket. She placed the bundle on the ground behind the almirah.

"There, that's better. No one can see her and it's away from the draught," she said and ran out of the house with my aunt.

My father bolted the door and we rushed into the jungle.

There was no time to send a message to the army camp on the other side of the village. It was too far away anyway and would take about half an hour for anyone to get there even on a bicycle. Besides, the Tamil terrorists were approaching from the side where the road turned off towards the direction of the army camp. Whoever it was that went to inform the army would be attacked instantly. They would never make it even halfway. Everyone else from the village was already running into the jungle. It was deep undergrowth. Everything looked dry and parched. Even the trees looked tired. We hid ourselves on trees and under bushes and waited silently for the terrorists to pass. We usually knew when they had left. They never stayed for more than a few hours as they were wary that the army might get wind of their presence. But we didn't come out for a long time; instead we waited until we were very sure they had left.

Once the people in another village returned to their homes only to find the terrorists had turned back as they has seen some army personnel approaching and were looking to hide in the village. The people had no time to rush back into the jungle. Every single one was slaughtered and left where they fell. Some died instantly while some lay dying for hours with no one to help. When the army was informed, it was too late. They were all dead. Since then we never came out until we felt certain the terrorists had left completely. Sometimes we waited the whole day. Hunger set in but we had learnt to ignore the gripping of our stomachs and suppress the noises of hunger in case even these small sounds acted as a giveaway.

The jungle took up most of the space in this tiny village. It stretched out as far as the eye could see. It started somewhere behind the old man's house beyond the well at the back of our garden and lost itself in the horizon. I had been here many times. It was the only place that was safe for us when the Tamil terrorists came looking for fun. There wouldn't be any school for all of us today either. The teachers had got used to the absence of students without notice. It was part of the life in this area. You got to live only if you were lucky. That seemed to be the way things were. The jungle used to be home to wild-cats, boar and snakes; wild elephants roamed on their way to their traditional watering holes. But today there were fewer wild animals. We had stopped being afraid of the wild animals. The only animals we were scared of were the humans in tiger stripes with guns and machetes that killed mercilessly. They didn't care that we were innocent farmers, mostly old people and children and women. They hated all of us because we were different, belonged to a different race from theirs. They saw us as being unfit to live. We were afraid of them, more afraid than the wild elephants that destroyed the vegetable gardens and the houses that stood in the path of the elephants. A wild elephant you could reason with, but not a terrorist.

The army had set up a camp to protect us but there was only so much they too could do. They were fighting the terrorists at the other end of the district, many villages from where we were. The small army camp did routine checks, but the terrorists hid and attacked from afar. They never showed their faces to the army but hid behind villages like cowards and attacked during the night. It was only when the army wasn't around that they showed their faces in the village, but none of the villagers carried a gun to protect themselves with, and it was an unequal relationship. Instead the villagers did the next best thing – they ran and hid in the jungle where the terrorists couldn't find them.

I saw the smoke from someone's hearth rising in the distance. It was the time when everyone prepared breakfast. No one had eaten as yet and the cooking hearths were left burning as we all ran for cover. I was hiding on a tree, sitting on a branch and holding onto another branch that passed overhead. Samanmali was sitting on the branch higher up. From my perch up here I could see my mother and aunt hiding between two bushes. An old woman from one of the neighboring houses was squatting nearby. The men were all standing behind bushes and encircling the group. The carried knives and large sticks – the only defense they had to protect the old, the women, the children and themselves. A few lookouts were posted on the trees in the vicinity. It was a blessing that the jungle was so thick with trees and bushes even though they were dried out. Where else would we have gone? I silently repeated a verse from one of the Buddha's sutras my mother chanted as she offered flowers to the Buddha image in our home. It was a protective verse and was all I remembered. I repeated it over and over and hoped the terrorists wouldn't come looking for us.

We must have stayed like that, silent, unmoving, listening, in fear, for ages. The sun had moved and was directly overhead and the heat was coursing through the undergrowth. No breeze blew in this harsh place. No birds sang. There was absolute silence. Even the rumblings of our stomachs had ceased. My throat was dry and my arms ached from holding onto the branch, but I dared not move in case the terrorists were someplace close and came to investigate the source of the noise. A single sound and we would all be dead. That was why we had to keep quiet and wait like statues, unmoving, unfeeling. I must have hidden like this many times. I stopped counting after the twentieth time. I think we must have hidden in the jungle more times than I ever went to school. Samanmali who always disagreed with anything I said didn't contradict me when I mentioned this to our mother one day. Instead she gave me a strange look and turned the other way.

Voices in the distance made us all tense. Was it the terrorists come looking for us? We held our breath and waited. After a while someone in the group spoke and we relaxed. The voices we heard were from the men standing watch. The message was passed down to us that it was now safe to return to the village. The terrorists had moved on. We came out of hiding and made our way back to the village as silently as we left. We had learnt that silence was the key to survival. That and vigilance.

The village was as we left it. It was as if nothing had happened, as if we hadn't left at all. The smoke rising from the fires in the houses had long stopped. The hearths had probably gone cold. We hurried back, thinking of the roti in the kitchen. The walk back from the jungle seemed like a long distance although it took us longer to get there and find a place to hide than it did for us to return. My father unlocked the door and we walked inside. The house had been turned upside down. They must have entered through the back door. We stared in dismay at our books lying on the floor. The tray of flowers placed in front of the Buddha image was under a chair and the flowers were scattered all around. The Buddha image was also on the ground. The head had been crushed and there were splinters on the body as if it was dashed on the ground. The kitchen too was in disarray. There was a strange smell that we couldn't quite place. We heard cries of dismay from Charulatha's mother in the next house. The terrorists seemed to have messed up their house too.

"They've eaten all our food," Charulatha's mother exclaimed.

Our rotis too were gone. The plate piled high with rotis was empty and the earthenware pot used to prepare the dhal was thrown to the corner of the kitchen. The fire in the hearth was burning low and the roti plate was still on it. But there was something else instead of the roti that my mother left on it to cook. A bundle in light pink turned charcoal black sat smoldering on the roti plate. It lay flat on the plate, silent, unmoving, the color of cinder. My mother fainted and fell to the ground in front of the hearth. The face that looked out from within the folds of the burnt fabric was etched in pain like I had never seen. It was like watching the dried leaves from the Sepalika tree after the flowers had faded in the noon sun. I screamed and fell to the ground next to my mother.

Many years later I came to Colombo to earn a living. My father was too old to work in the fields. He lost his leg to a landmine and could only hobble around. Samanmali helped in the house but she too would leave soon to live in her husband's house in a place that was not so fearful. My parents would be left to fend for themselves. The money I earned would help them now that they were old. It would also help me to continue with my studies at the university. It was a different life here; not at all like the life in the village. It felt strange to think that I came from a place like my village that these people here had not heard about. They were sympathetic towards our way of life, but didn't really understand. They were horrified at the things we had to live through and couldn't quite believe their ears. They wanted to help, but were as helpless as I was. More helpless as they didn't even understand the way of our life in that small village so far away from anything anyone knew. But they were kind. The house I was boarded at was small and I shared a room with two others. It was not too uncomfortable and the people running the place were kind. I liked this house. It reminded me of my home in the village. Whenever I felt homesick I sat under the tree with the tiny white flowers and orange stems whose name I could no longer say. It was the same tree that stood at the front of my home in the village. I can never forget that day when I was small, as long as I see the little flowers or the shape of the tree. I closed my eyes and said a silent prayer to all those that I missed.

# About the Author

Shirani Rajapakse is a Sri Lankan poet and author. She won the *Cha "Betrayal" Poetry Contest 2013* and was a finalist in the *Anna Davidson Rosenberg Poetry Awards 2013.*

Her debut collection of short stories, *Breaking News* (Vijitha Yapa 2011) was shortlisted for the *Gratiaen Award.* Her critically acclaimed poetry collection *Chant of a Million Women* (self published 2017) won the *2018 Kindle Book Awards.* It received an Honorable Mention in the *2018 Readers' Favorite Awards* and was chosen as an "Official Selection" in the *2018 New Apple Summer eBook Awards for Excellence in Independent Publishing. I Exist. Therefore I Am* (self-published 2018) is her second collection of short stories.

Rajapakse's work appears in many international publications including, *Flash:The International Short-Short Story Magazine, Litro, Silver Birch, International Times, City Journal, Writers for Calais Refugees, The Write-In, Asian Signature, Moving Worlds, Citiesplus, Deep Water Literary Journal, Mascara Literary Review, Kitaab, Lakeview Journal, Cyclamens & Swords, New Ceylon Writing, Channels, Linnet's Wings, Spark, Berfrois, Counterpunch, Earthen Lamp Journal, Asian Cha, Dove Tales, Buddhist Poetry Review, About Place Journal, Skylight 47, The Smoking Poet, New Verse News, The Occupy Poetry Project* and in anthologies, *Fireflies & Fairy Dust: A Fantasy Anthology (Eu-2 2018), Flash*

*Fiction International (Norton 2015), Ballads (Dagda 2014), Short & Sweet (Perera Hussein 2014), Poems for Freedom (River Books 2013), Voices Israel Poetry Anthology 2012, Song of Sahel (Plum Tree 2012), Occupy Wall Street Poetry Anthology, World Healing World Peace (Inner City Press 2012 & 2014)* and *Every Child Is Entitled to Innocence (Plum Tree 2012).*

Rajapakse has a BA in English Literature (University of Kelaniya, Sri Lanka) and MA in International Relations (Jawaharlal Nehru University, India). She worked as a journalist, researcher and an international development specialist before becoming a creative writer. An animal lover and vegetarian she loves to travel. Rajapakse lives in the suburbs of Sri Lanka's capital Colombo.

# Thanks for reading!

Please add a short review on Amazon, Goodreads, your personal blog or any other book related site and let me know what you thought about the book.

My second collection of short stories, *I Exist. Therefore I Am* is out now. It's set in India and is about women. Or, if you prefer poetry, check out the critically acclaimed *Chant of a Million Women* (self-published, 2017). It won the *2018 Kindle Book Awards* received an Honorable Mention in the *2018 Readers' Favorite Awards 2018* and was chosen as an Official Selection in the *2018 New Apple Summer eBook Awards for Excellence in Independent Publishing.*

shiranirajapakse.wordpress.com
amazon.com/Shirani-Rajapakse/e/B00IZQRAOA